A Misanthrope Teaches a Class for Demi-Humans

Mr. Hitoma, Won't You Teach Us About Humans...?

Kurusu Natsume   Illustration by **Sai Izumi**

The Principal

Yuki Saotome

Satoru Hoshino

Tobari Haneda

Rei Hitoma

Isaki Oogami

Kyouka Minazuki

Sui Usami

CHARACTERS

At last, the long-awaited summer! Blue skies! White clouds! And my pasty self!

Half dozing atop a vinyl sheet with my head pillowed on my bag, I watched the students play around in the water.

A Nonhuman
Girl's Pride

"I do not
need
help."

KYOUKA MINAZUKI

TOBARI HANEDA

REI HITOMA

SUI USAMI

ISAKI OOGAMI

A MISANTHROPE TEACHES A CLASS FOR DEMI-HUMANS

A Misanthrope
Teaches a Class for
Demi-Humans

Mr. Hitoma, Won't You Teach Us About Humans...?

Kurusu Natsume

Illustration by
Sai Izumi

New York

A MISANTHROPE TEACHES A CLASS FOR DEMI-HUMANS

A Misanthrope

Teaches a Class for

Demi-Humans

(1)

Kurusu Natsume

Illustration by
Sai Izumi

Translation by Linda Liu
Cover art by Sai Izumi

JINGAIKYOSHITSU NO NINGENGIRAIKYOSHI Vol. 1
HITOMASENSEI, WATASHITACHI NI NINGEN O OSHIETEKUREMASUKA......?
©Kurusu Natsume 2022 ©2022 ANYCOLOR, Inc.
First published in Japan in 2022 by KADOKAWA CORPORATION, Tokyo.
English translation rights arranged with KADOKAWA CORPORATION,
Tokyo, through TUTTLE-MORI AGENCY, INC., Tokyo.

English translation © 2023 by Yen Press, LLC

Yen On
150 West 30th Street, 19th Floor
New York, NY 10001

Visit us at yenpress.com • facebook.com/yenpress • twitter.com/yenpress
yenpress.tumblr.com • instagram.com/yenpress

First Yen On Edition: October 2023
Edited by Yen On Editorial: Rachel Mimms
Designed by Yen Press Design: Eddy Mingki

Yen On is an imprint of Yen Press, LLC.
The Yen On name and logo are trademarks of Yen Press, LLC.

Library of Congress Cataloging-in-Publication Data
Names: Kurusu, Natsume, 2000- author. | Izumi, Sai, illustrator. | Liu,
Linda (Translator), translator.
Title: A misanthrope teaches a class for demi-humans / Kurusu Natsume ;
illustration by Sai Izumi ; translated by Linda Liu.
Other titles: Jingaikyoshitsu no ningengiraikyoshi. English
Description: New York : Yen On, 2023- |
Contents: v. 1. Mr. Hitoma, won't you teach us about humans...? —
Identifiers: LCCN 2023028672 | ISBN 9781975371050 (v. 1 ; trade paperback) |
ISBN 9781975371074 (v. 2 ; trade paperback)
Subjects: CYAC: Fantasy. | Schools—Fiction. | Identity—Fiction. | LCGFT:
Fantasy fiction. | Light novels.
Classification: LCC PZ7.1.N3735 Mi 2023 | DDC [Fic]—dc23
LC record available at https://lccn.loc.gov/2023028672

ISBNs: 978-1-9753-7105-0 (paperback)
978-1-9753-7106-7 (ebook)

10 9 8 7 6 5 4 3 2 1

LSC-C

Printed in the United States of America

Humans—I *hate* humans.

They're selfish. Uncaring about others.

They exploit the good in bad faith and take the honest as fools.

And yeah, I used to be one of those fools.

I don't have the power to change a thing, not a one. There's no point in trying.

I hate—

"Mr. Hitoma? Hello? What are you zoning out for all of a sudden?"

A girl's slightly husky voice brought me back to my senses.

This was a classroom. I was overlooking my students from the podium.

Dark-brown pillars cut across the white walls. It was an elegant, vintage-style room.

Before me were four girls, each with animal ears or wings.

"Tobari, it's Mr. Hitoma's first day here! He must be tired."

"Whaaa—? You think? I bet he was daydreaming about something stupid!"

"Agreed. Just look at his face—he's thinking scummy thoughts."

"Y-you two shouldn't speak that way to our teacher... Ohhh..."

Watching these outspoken girls left me feeling slightly on edge.

"...Um...Mr. Hitoma...?"

"Check out that grin on his face."

I hurried to wipe off the smile that had gotten away from me. "No, that's not— Sorry, never mind."

"Ah, I know. You must've been mesmerized by our charm, right, Mr. Hitoma?"

"Oh my! But I can sympathize! Tobari's blue eyes, Usami's long ears, and Isaki's fluffy tail—and I'm quite charming, too, if I do say so myself! Of course, that's not all there is to us!"

"A-ah... My tail... I appreciate the compliment...!"

It was as if I'd been reincarnated in another world.

These girls weren't human.
And yet, they admired humans more than anyone.

These are the praises sung of humans by nonhumans, the story I bore witness to in my tenure as their teacher.

A MISANTHROPE TEACHES A
CLASS FOR DEMI-HUMANS

CONTENTS

Prologue

"Score! Eighteen kills! Go, go, go, go!!"

Am I gonna beat my personal record—?!

"Raaaaaaaah!!!!"

Just then, my mom slammed open the door to my room.

"Stop yelling! It's the middle of the night! You're gonna wake the whole neighborhood!!"

Startled, I accidentally dropped the controller when my hand slipped.

"Arghhh!!!!"

In the next moment, one word was splashed across the screen, merciless and brutal:

Annihilated

"Noooooo... I almost had it..."

"This isn't the time for that," my mom chided. "You can't just play your games all the time. What happened to your talk of job searching?!"

Not this again...

I placed the controller back on my desk, fed up.

"Yeah, I'll get to it..."

Exasperated, my mom heaved her usual deep sigh. "You always say that... It's been two years already..."

Two years ago, I had been a teacher. I'd worked at a high school in the city for four years after landing the job straight out of teachers' college.

Until the incident.

"That's right—Mitsuko called today." Oblivious to my walk down memory lane, my mom switched gears to family gossip. Mitsuko was my mom's younger sister—my aunt. "You remember your cousin Nat! She's in Bolivia now. She directs traffic in a zebra costume!"

"Oh, that's neat... Wait—Nat's doing what now?!" I blurted out despite myself. The craziness of what I'd just heard pushed the words out of my mouth.

This is the same Nat we're talking about, right? Sweet, gentle, reserved Nat? The hell? Is this a joke?

"Heh-heh, I'm sure people will heed any warnings if they're given by a cute zebra traffic cop," my mom said with a chuckle. "Anyway, what I'm trying to say is: There are plenty of jobs in the world. What about your future? Any luck with the job search?"

"Welllll, here and there..."

That was a lie. My search was going nowhere.

"Listen to me, Rei-Rei—"

I really wish she'd stop with the pet name. I'm almost thirty years old.

"—your father is going to retire next year. Our family's going to be in a tough position if you don't start working soon. Don't you want to teach anymore?"

"Teach..."

To tell the truth, I hadn't hated my job as a teacher. I enjoyed seeing my students grow and mature.

"I don't want to interfere too much with your life, but...sweetie...I'm your mother, and I just want you to know that I'm worried about you."

With that, she left my room.

Her kind words stoked my guilt.

Any mother would be worried if their only son spent all his time holed up at home and gaming...

My mom had worn the same rueful expression she always did. I wanted to reassure her everything would be all right, but being the coward I was, I didn't yet have the courage to take the next step.

Two years ago, my mom had witnessed me stumble home day after day, my spirit in tatters. Back then, I was barely eating. I lost interest in my beloved games. Every day, I got home and collapsed into bed, my battery completely drained. Even when I was able to catch a bit of sleep, I would inevitably wake up again, so I wasn't able to recover at all. The night would pass, and dawn would break. Then, resenting the stabbing rays of the morning sun, I would down an energy drink and drag myself to work.

Now, my appetite was back to normal, and gaming was fun again. I still didn't sleep well, but you can't win them all. My current lifestyle was much healthier than back in those days.

"A new job... Mm..."

I opened a job-search site on the laptop in front of me.

"Sales...is out of the question... And customer service feels like a bad fit for me..."

Ever since I quit teaching, I would every once in a while repeat this cycle of opening and closing job sites. I bookmarked a few postings each time but never got around to applying for them.

Rinse and repeat.

A job worth doing? What did that even mean?

Fulfillment! Growth! Sense of accomplishment!

Similar phrases were lined up ad infinitum on such sites.

"Aaah, a cozy workplace would be nice..."

All right, today I'll bookmark a few jobs by the shore or mountains, and then I'll go to sleep!

I scrolled through the search results.

That was when I saw this listing:

Wanted: All-Girls Private School Teacher! Let the tranquil mountain atmosphere rejuvenate you as you work.

A school.

Possessed by god knows what, I found myself clicking on the DETAILS link.

Licensed High School Teacher (Social Studies, Language Arts, Fine Arts, Home Economics)

Full-time Employment
Salary: ¥500,000 to ¥850,000 per month
Bonus: Six-month lump sum paid twice per year (based on performance)
Social security provided. On-campus housing. Natural hot spring on site.
Cherry blossom viewing in the spring and matsutake mushroom foraging in the fall?! This is one nature-filled, rejuvenating workplace you won't want to miss! Fantasy lovers welcome! Humanlike applicants welcome! At our school, we respect sincerity and autonomy! Our ideal candidate is a teacher who puts their students first! ♪ Do you want to grow alongside your students? Then please apply! We look forward to your application!!

Woooooooooow...
Sketchy as all hell...
Laughing at the overtly shady job description, I scrolled through the photos of the school. That's when the nostalgia came welling up from deep within my heart.

My life as a teacher had come to a close two years ago, leaving me with bitter memories.

But there had been fun times, too.

The school in the photos was nestled in the mountains, lit by soft sunlight filtering through the trees. It looked like a place that could blow all one's problems away.

The ideal candidate... A teacher who puts their students first...
Quintessential phrases in job listings.
Yet, for some reason, that two-bit line hooked me.

There must be something wrong with me. There must be.
This weird listing was getting to my head.
That was all it was.

Before I realized it, I'd already clicked the APPLY button.

* * *

Shiranui Private High School.

That was the name of the school that had posted that bizarre job listing.

The kanji that made up its name didn't look like they would be read as Shiranui. According to the school's overview, it was the name of the board director.

After my inadvertent application, I flew through the interview process: application review, written examination, mock lesson, interview.

And then:

"Rei-Rei! You actually looked for a job!" My mom was ecstatic. "I was shocked when I went through the mail today! Look! Offer of Employment! It's written right here! How do you read the school name? Fushibi…? Fushibi Private High School? It's from a high school! A school… Ohhh… Good work, Rei-Rei!"

Somehow, I had landed a job offer from Shiranui Private High School.

April 1, my first day on the new job.

The entire interview process had been conducted remotely, so it was my first time visiting the school. To get there, I had to take a train and then a bus. The whole trip took an hour and a half.

"…You can't be serious."

I stepped off the bus into nature even more lush and wild than I'd been picturing. There wasn't a single building or any recognizable roads in sight. I'd double- and triple-checked the name of the nearest bus stop on my way here. I was definitely in the right place…I was pretty sure.

I ruffled through the envelope of documents the school had sent in search of the map.

Just then, I noticed a small orange envelope tucked into the larger one. *What's this? Has this always been here?*

I pinched the envelope between my fingers. There was something hard in it. I opened it up and removed its contents.

Tucked inside was a small silver ring embedded with a red stone, along with a sticky note.

Dear Mr. Rei Hitoma,
Please make sure to wear this ring on your left finger when you come to the school.

"Huh...?"

I didn't understand what for. Plus, it seemed like a pain. Nevertheless, I did as the note instructed and slid the ring on. It fit my left pinkie perfectly.

I took out the map from the document envelope. It indicated that the school could be reached by following a road leading off from the bus stop. A short ways down that path, there should be a large cherry blossom tree that served as a landmark.

What road? I don't see any—

There it is.

I glanced up from the map. Right in front of me was a road two meters wide.

A gentle breeze was blowing. I could see the cherry blossom tree in the distance, too.

Why didn't I see it earlier? I didn't notice anything before I took out the map. Sure, the road isn't paved, but it's definitely an actual road. There's no way I could've missed it...

No, I probably just overlooked it because I was distracted by the giant forest.

I'm not used to the commute, and I haven't traveled so far from home in a long time. I'm sure I'm just tired.

A little ways into the forest, I spotted the school.

As pictured on the map, the grounds were massive, but the school buildings themselves were on the smaller side. According to the documents I'd received, there weren't many students, either.

As I drew closer, I noticed a tall, slim man standing in front of what must have been the main entrance. He was wearing glasses and appeared to be in his midthirties.

A veteran teacher, maybe?

He was stooped over, reading a book.

I stared at him for a while before his gaze snapped up to meet mine.

"Ah, Mr. Hitoma...right?" he asked.

"Oh—! Uh...i-it's a pleasure to make your acquaintance," I stammered. "My name is Rei Hitoma, and I will be working here starting today."

A warm, friendly smile rose to the man's face. "We've heard. You're the new social studies teacher, right? Welcome to Shiranui High. I'm Satoru Hoshino. I teach math. Anyway...you don't need to be so formal. This school's a bit peculiar, which might be hard to get used to in its own way, but I'm here to help with whatever you need. Just speak up. I'll help you get settled in your job and be your tour guide today. The principal asked me to."

"Oh, I see. Thank you very much."

Mr. Hoshino handed me a pair of guest slippers. I put them on, and we headed inside.

The interior featured a brown-and-white color scheme with decorative accents that looked like they were taken straight from a fantasy story. It was exactly like the pictures I'd seen on the job-search site and in the school documents.

Hmm? Those weren't in the photos.

In front of me were bottles. Lots and lots of bottles.

The small, glittering bottles were packed tightly together right by the front entrance.

"Pretty, aren't they?" Mr. Hoshino said, following my gaze.

"Ah, I'm sorry. What are these for?" I asked.

"Hmm. They're a distinct feature of this school, you could say."

"A feature?"

I didn't understand what Mr. Hoshino was getting at. Were my comprehension skills lacking? But if they were something special, I should've remembered them from the school materials...

My expression must have given away my confusion.

"It's a long explanation, you see," Mr. Hoshino added, scratching his cheek awkwardly. "I think I'll just confuse you if I try. Sorry."

"Oh! Please don't worry! I apologize for prying!"

I was still lost, but that didn't seem like it'd be a problem. I wondered if someone was going to explain the bottles to me later on.

"And here is the teachers' office."

Mr. Hoshino's voice snapped me out of my idle musing about the school.

The room was on the second floor, right next to the stairs leading up from the entrance. Mr. Hoshino gestured for me to open the door. I slid it open.

"I apologize for the disturbance..."

I looked around the room with wide eyes. My gaze landed on a pretty young woman with long hair falling neatly down her back. She wore a long white coat over her business-casual outfit.

She was working at her desk, but when she noticed the two of us standing at the door, she stopped what she was doing and scampered toward us like a small animal.

"Ah! Mr. Hoshinooo! Could this be the new teacher?!"

Oh man, she's...a-adorable!

"G-good morning. My name is Rei Hitoma, and I will be working here starting today. It's a pleasure to meet you."

"Likewise! I'm Yuki Saotome. I'm in charge of Culinary Arts! The students all call me Ms. Yuki! Feel free to call me that, too, Mr. Hitoma!" Ms. Yuki—or Ms. Saotome, to be proper—flashed a dazzling smile, her head held high with pride.

Ms. Saotome was so beautiful, she seemed like she was a different species. Her eyes were large and clear, her hair silky and lustrous, and her physique slim and toned. Her sweet and soft, bell-like voice was the cherry on top.

"Let's see...your seat is over there, Mr. Hitoma, by the windows at the end." Mr. Hoshino pointed to the desk in question. "Your bag must be heavy. Why don't you put it down for now?"

"Thank you."

I excused myself to Ms. Saotome and turned to do as directed.

But right as I was about to pass Ms. Saotome, her hand darted out to grab my sleeve.

"Oh, hold on a second, Mr. Hitoma."

"Whoa—!" I yelped as she leaned in close, bringing her lovely face next to mine. "Um, w-wait!!"

"...Sorry, can you hold still for a moment?" she said, looking up at me, drawing even closer.

A pleasant, mellow scent hit my nose.

Is that her shampoo? Or does Ms. Saotome herself smell this good?

My head was spinning. Ms. Saotome lifted a hand and placed it on... my cheek. Her touch was cooler than I had anticipated.

"Ummmm, e-excuse me, Ms. Saotome...!!"

Overwhelmed by the close proximity, I was about to bolt when...

"Yes! Got it!!"

Ms. Saotome's giddy voice rang through the teachers' office. In her hand was a small black hair.

"Mr. Hitoma! There was an eyelash on your cheek!"

Eyelash?! She could've at least warned me first!

"Ah, um, I'm sorry for the inconvenience, Ms. Saotome! Thank you very much...!" I fumbled frantically through my bag for a tissue and handed it to her.

"...Um, Ms. Yuki?" Mr. Hoshino interjected. He'd been watching our interaction from the sidelines. "I think it'd be best for you not to do things like that."

"Oh, ah, Mr. Hoshino... I'm sorry. It just happened to catch my eye..."

"What's done is done." He sighed. "Restrain yourself next time, all right?"

Mr. Hoshino sat down in the seat next to the one he'd pointed out as mine.

I walked over to my desk and looked around the room from a fresh vantage point.

It'd been a while since I'd last laid eyes on a place like this.

Here in the teachers' office was my own personal space. This felt so familiar.

"Mr. Hitoma, the principal is waiting for you." Mr. Hoshino pointed to a door farther into the room. "Drop off your bag and go introduce yourself."

"All right. Thank you."

I made my way to the principal's office.

The principal...

My interview with him, like the rest of the process, had been conducted online, so I was meeting him for the first time in person.

If I remembered correctly, the principal was a tall man. During the interview, he'd been wearing an expensive but subdued suit. Other than that...what had left a vivid impression on me was the sparkling monocle that had been perched over one eye. To me, monocles were the stuff of detective manga and light novels. I distinctly recalled thinking at the time, *I guess real people wear them, too...*

I knocked on the door. "Come in," a man called from inside.

"Pardon me."

I eased the door open.

The principal's office was arrayed with upscale furnishings and decorations. The man himself stood by the window with his back toward me.

True to my memory, he had a tall stature and slim physique that rivaled Mr. Hoshino's. He was wearing a refined gray suit and was looking out the window with his hands laced behind his back.

"Hello. We met over video during the interview, but please allow me to reintroduce myself. My name is Rei Hitoma, and I will be in charge of social studies from today forward. Thank you for this honor."

Once I recited my self-introduction, I bowed to the principal.

He said nothing.

Maybe he didn't hear me?

"Please let me reintroduce myself! My name is Rei Hitoma. I'll be teaching social studies from today on! Thank you for this honor!" I repeated, louder than before.

But again, I received no response. The principal carried on staring out the window without so much as batting an eye. He was more like a corpse than a living, breathing human being.

I gathered my resolve and approached him.

"Excuse me? I apologize if I've offended you in some way. For my edification and future reference, would you be so kind as to inform me what I did wrong—? Agh!!"

I really had been talking to—to a corpse this whole time!

No, wait, this is—

"A w-wax figure?"

"Ding, ding, ding! Youuuuuuuuu win!!!!"
"Uwaaaaaaaaaaaah!!!!"

Suddenly, a boulder of a man burst out of the shadow behind the door and came barreling toward me. Startled, I slipped and landed flat on my butt.

What's happening?! Or rather—who in the world?!

The rotund entity that had charged me turned out to be a stout man, who was gaudy in every sense of the word.

Wh—?! Don't tell me… Is this the director?!

I'd seen neither hide nor hair of the director yet. Only their name was printed on the school pamphlet. They'd been absent during my interview, so the principal had taken over those duties.

The man in front of me was heavyset and plump. He was wearing a yellow suit and a small hat. He had curly hair, a beard, and round eyes—plus, one of those eyes sported a sparkling gold-rimmed monocle. And on his shoulder was a small…bird?

I was still sitting where I'd fallen. The portly man smiled warmly and extended a hand to help me up.

"Welcome, my boy! ♪ I believe I last had the pleasure of meeting you during your interview. I'm the principal, Karasuma!"

"Like I'd believe that!" He was very obviously a different person from the principal I'd met. "Then tell me, what the hell is that wax figure?! What happened to the tall, sophisticated principal from the interview?! You're the polar opposite of him! This prank isn't funny!"

Faced with my utter incomprehension of the situation, the self-proclaimed principal lowered his hand dejectedly.

"Mm, it's only natural that you find me suspicious." He turned on his heel and sat in a chair in the middle of the room. "First, I'll explain my appearance in the interview. Come over here and take a seat, my boy."

I got to my feet and wobbled to the chair—fully leather and expensive-looking—opposite him as instructed.

The mysterious principal—again, self-declared—resumed speaking.

"Now then, the me you met during the interview—that was a substitute."

"Uh-huh…"

"My illusory magic makes it so that candidates who will be a good fit for this school see me as a tall, striking man. That's how we know that they'll be compatible with the school's barrier."

Say what now?

Illusions? Barriers? Has he been reading too much fantasy?

"I don't know if you remember," the principal said, "but at the beginning of the interview, I asked you about my appearance."

I remembered.

They'd been trivial questions about his suit and looks. I'd assumed he did it to soothe my nerves.

"As it turns out, that question makes or breaks the hiring decision."

"…*That's* how you decide who passes?"

"Oh, of course we factor in the mock lesson and exam, too!"

They hire people based on their susceptibility to hypnosis?

No, no, no, back up. What exactly is this magic he's talking about?

"Okay! Let me explain why the illusions are necessary to the employment process! The answer is that this school is home to—drumroll please!—marvelous and very special students!"

"'Special'…?"

"That's right. In short, nonhuman students."

Nonhuman.

Did I mishear?

"Um, uh… Excuse me, but what do you mean by that?"

I was overwhelmed, but I pressed forward nonetheless.

Was a fantasy world about to unfold before my very eyes?

"Demi-human children—be they mermaids or aviary in nature, dragon or panda, canine or feline—gather at this school to learn how to become human, each with their own unique goals."

…Turned out I was spot-on about the fantasy stuff.

Mermaids and birds and dragons…?

"I'll now explain to you the truth about Shiranui High School, as well as the terms of your employment."

* * *

Here's a summary of the following hour or so of my conversation with the principal:

- About the school
  - This is a school for nonhuman students.
  - Every student who attends this school has their own personal goal, the achievement of which requires them to learn to be human.
  - The curriculum comprises three main parts: General Education, Human Nature & Humanity, and Society & Communication.

- o General Education teaches knowledge and information needed to survive in human society. It is graded through exams.
- o Human Nature & Humanity teaches students to behave, emote, and think the way humans do. Students are measured on how humanlike they are. The school—the teachers, for all intents and purposes—can dock points for unhuman-like behavior and for rule violations. These scores are reflected on the students' transcripts.
- o Society & Communication teaches group work, social skills such as interpersonal connections and compromise, and courtesy such as showing respect and consideration toward others. Students are graded on their sociability through a unique method: a student-to-student voting system.
- o Votes relating to Human Nature & Humanity and Society & Communication can be submitted at any time using each individual student's bottle found next to the school entrance *(the ones I saw when I was with Mr. Hoshino)*. Points are collected in these bottles.

- Terms of employment
  - o The term of the contract is three years, after which the contract can be renewed or terminated.
  - o Bonuses of up to a half year's portion are paid out twice a year based on performance.
  - o An additional twelve-month bonus is given upon completion of the full term or contract renewal.
  - o If the contract is terminated at the end of the term, the school can assist with locating a next employer in line with the contractee's preferences, based on their relationship with the school.
  - o Should the contract be terminated for any reason before the term is up, the contractee's memories of working at this school will be replaced with dummy memories of working at a different, regular school.

Taking into account the base salary and various subsidiaries, the terms were just as good as, if not better than, the ones listed on the fishy job listing. I was happy, but…it seemed too good to be true.

What did "nonhuman students" actually mean?

How much of what he was telling me was real…?

The principal shot to his feet.

"Seeing is believing, as they say! Come, my boy. Let's take a walk down to the student dorm!"

"Uh, right now?!"

"Of course! Going in might be difficult, but we should at least be able to take a peek from a distance!"

…Was it that obvious that I was skeptical?

Just like that, I was whisked away by the principal on a tour of the dorms.

* * *

From the main building, the student dorms were apparently some distance west through the forest.

The principal plodded along the trail in front of me. "Not long now, my boy."

The road weaved through the trees. I heard the faint sound of girls laughing.

We arrived at the dorm, which shared a similar design with the school building.

"Ah! Principal Karasuma! Good to see you!" someone shouted from above us. "Is that the new teacher you mentioned?!"

I looked in the direction the voice was coming from and saw a hardy woman drying sheets on the roof. I also caught glimpses of girls bustling around her.

"That's right!" the principal yelled back. "This is the newbie, Rei Hitoma!"

"Oh yeah? Mr. Hitoma? Did I get that right? Nice to meetcha! I'm the dorm mom! I take care of the students! The name's Ryouko Shinonome! Roost Rep Ryouko—that's how you can remember it!"

"Oh! I'm Rei Hitoma! Pleased to meet you!" I shouted.

When was the last time I yelled at the top of my lungs outdoors?

Ryouko waved her hand over her head before returning to drying sheets with the girls who I assumed were students.

The girls had animal features like big rabbit ears or long tails...
At first, I thought it was cosplay, but even from a distance, I could tell.

They were the real deal.
The students really were nonhuman...

Nonhuman...
I didn't know why, but having seen the truth with my own eyes, I felt my shoulders slump.

"It's time we headed back to my office," said the principal.

I followed him back along the road. My body moved on autopilot; my head had yet to catch up.

"Do you believe me?"

I didn't know how to answer him. I could only stare back in silence.

His gaze dropped down to my hand. "Ah, I see that you're wearing the ring."

Ring? Oh, the one that came with the school materials.

"This ring uses one of the director's gems. It's a very special ring," he continued.

"Special...?"

"We like to make sure regular folks can't find this school, you see! That's why we've cast a notice-me-not spell over the road from the bus stop! On top of that, the director's barrier extends all the way to the cherry tree! The ring on your finger nullifies the magic and makes it as if you are already part of the barrier."

Notice-me-not spell and a barrier...

I get it now. The spell's effect was why I hadn't been able to find the road to the school when I first got off at the bus stop.

A question leaped to the fore of my mind.

"This ring... What will happen if I remove it right now? Will I be ejected from the barrier...?"

The principal's round eyes widened even further. "N-nothing so dramatic! You can take off the ring inside the barrier, and it won't have much of an effect. You'll still be able to leave if you want. However, you'll be in a pinch if you leave the barrier without the ring on or if you take it off outside the barrier's bounds."

"What do you mean…?"

"Your memories of this school will vanish."

"They'll what…?!"

That's terrifying…!

What the hell? The consequences were far more absurd than I'd imagined.

"That's right. If you remove the ring outside, you'll forget everything about this school, and your memories will be replaced by false ones. That's why you should keep the ring on your person at all times! But accidents happen! And if one does, your memories will return if you touch the ring again. So don't worry!"

"I see…"

I stared intently at the ring around my finger.

As a man, wearing a ring is a little…

Granted, it didn't look much different from a wedding ring. I'd originally planned to remove it once I was off campus, but now that I knew about the dire consequences, I would definitely not be doing that.

"One more thing," the principal added. "The students wear these rings during extracurriculars as well."

"They do?"

"Yes. The students appear as demi-humans thanks to the director's barrier. But their true identities aren't human but dogs or cats or dragons. That's why, should they leave the barrier, they'll return to their regular selves… However! With this wonderful ring, they'll be able to remain in their demi-human form outside just as they do at school!"

I see.

In other words, the students appeared the way they did because of the director's power.

Just who or what is this director…?

"That's a wrap on my spiel about the school!"

The principal was walking a few paces ahead of me. He stopped and spun around to face me. We'd circled back to the front entrance of the main building as we talked.

"Rei Hitoma. This is the last time I'll ask you this. This school is not, in a word, normal. All our students have a personal reason for wanting to become human, and this is where they strive to accomplish their goal. You're likely to find that your responsibilities here are heavier than they would be at the average high school."

Suddenly, the principal's mood shifted.

"Knowing all of that, will you still stay to teach the students at this school?"

…It was true that there were plenty of aspects about this school that I had yet to understand.

Compared to teaching at a run-of-the-mill school, working here, the weight on my shoulders would be heavier.

But I'd already come all this way.

It's a pain to look for yet another job. Besides, there's something exciting about this reincarnated-in-another-world kind of setting.

Plus, the salary was appropriately generous. Therefore:

"Yes, I will. I'm honored to be working with you going forward."

The principal smiled at me kindly.

The spring breeze brought the fragrance of cherry blossoms from places unseen, and the speckled sunlight falling through the trees warmed my face, shifting in response to the movement of the leaves rustling in the wind.

That day, my new life began.

This is neither a tale of another world nor of rebirth.

It's merely the story of a teacher's day-to-day life at a somewhat peculiar school.

A **Misanthrope**
Teaches a Class for
Demi-Humans

Mr. Hitoma, Won't You Teach Us About Humans...?

The Misanthrope and the
Classroom of Destiny

A MISANTHROPE TEACHES A CLASS FOR DEMI-HUMANS

After starting my new job on April 1, I spent the next few days leading up to the opening ceremony in a mad scramble. Against all odds, I had been assigned a homeroom class…!

The preparations overwhelmed me. Mr. Hoshino's and Ms. Saotome's support were my saving grace. Unable to bear watching me struggle, Mr. Hoshino and Ms. Saotome helped me with the paperwork and plied me with delicious coffee and cookies. You wouldn't be wrong to call it bribery, with the way they were doling out kindness like treats for a stray dog, but it was the first time I had been shown such consideration in the workplace.

During those helter-skelter days, my birthday on the third came and went, and I greeted the last year of my twenties…

Anyway, here are the particulars I learned about the school.

First, the student body wasn't divided into grades, since the number of years needed to graduate wasn't fixed. Instead, they were roughly split into beginner, intermediate, and advanced classes based on proficiency.

There were prerequisites to advance to the next level. The decision was made based on their performance on a special assignment given at the end of the school year and on their grades throughout the year. If they fulfilled the requirements, they moved up a class or graduated.

Some students were unable to meet the qualifications and stayed in the beginner class year after year. Other students dropped out. For that reason, the class size decreased from level to level.

Graduation:

When students graduated, they became human, left the school, and joined the broader human community. From there on, each student carried out their life as an individual human being in pursuit of their own goals.

I was going to be the homeroom teacher of the advanced class, the very students perched on the precipice of graduation. There was a grand total of four of them.

That day was the start of the new semester, and I was going to be meeting my students for the first time. I'd received their profiles beforehand, but to think I was actually going to meet them in person...

"Ughhh, my stomach hurts...," I moaned.

"Mr. Hitoma, hi! Are you feeling all right?"

"Ack! Ms. Saotome! I-I-I'm fine!!!"

"Oh, I must have startled you by talking to you out of nowhere! Sorry about that! By the way, you're older than me, right? That's what I figured. But you're my first junior at work! I get so excited thinking there's a newbie around, and before I know it, I'm already opening my mouth to talk to you!"

Ms. Saotome's smile pierced my heart. *I think the clenching pain in my chest might outperform the knots in my stomach...*

"Ah, the students should be arriving soon."

She was looking out the window with a soft smile. At the other end of her gaze were the students streaming toward the front entrance.

There was no prescribed school uniform here. Each student could pick what they wanted to wear as long as it was relatively formal. Some wore sailor uniforms, others wore blazers... There was a lack of cohesiveness, but on the other hand, the students' unique personalities shone through in their choices. As a teacher, as self-serving a reason as it might be, this made it easier for me to identify them.

"Well then, Mr. Hitoma, shall we head over to the gymnasium?"

"Ah, sure."

It was time for the opening ceremony. Given the small number of students, it doubled as an entrance ceremony, too.

I mentally chanted over and over again the self-introduction I'd prepared.

I'll be fine. It'll all be fine.

* * *

After the dreaded ceremony ended, I returned to the teachers' office with Ms. Saotome and Mr. Hoshino.

"Good work, Mr. Hitoma!" Ms. Saotome said.

"That was a great introduction," Mr. Hoshino told me.

"Th-thank you. I couldn't think of anything creative, though…"

"Oh, please! That's what made it so good!" Ms. Saotome reassured me.

"Exactly. There wasn't a single baseball metaphor. The principal puts them in every single speech."

"All of them?" I asked.

"Every! Single! One!" Ms. Saotome confirmed. "Last graduation, he talked about pick-off throws. This time, it was pop-ups to the catcher."

"He's a big fan…," Mr. Hoshino added.

"I don't know the first thing about the sport, but I've picked up all the lingo over the years! By the way, what about you, Mr. Hitoma? Any hobbies?"

"Um, errr, gaming, I guess…"

I was caught off guard with the question, and the truth slipped out of my mouth. *Damn.*

"Oooh! You like games!" Ms. Saotome exclaimed. "There's one I'm particularly good at, you know."

I didn't expect that…!

I played it cool, but inside, I was screaming.

"I'm a killer *hanafuda* player!" she declared proudly.

A fan of the classics. Cute!

Hmm… *Hanafuda…hanafuda…* The only memory I had of the game was being forced to play with relatives on New Year's.

"Ms. Yuki's a tough opponent," Mr. Hoshino told me. "You should try and play her once."

"Ah, I'd love to," I said.

"Heh-heh! Don't expect me to go easy on you! I'm a tough cookie!"

Her pouty expression was adorable.

While I was being revitalized by Ms. Saotome's loveliness, next to me, Mr. Hoshino seemed to have suddenly remembered something.

"Come to think of it, didn't you say you were a homeroom teacher in the past?" he asked. "What was your last school like?"

My blood ran cold, freezing with an audible crackle.

My last school.

A black shadow crept through my heart.

Mr. Hoshino hadn't done anything wrong. It was my fault for not being able to elegantly sidestep the question.

"My...last school was..."

I couldn't string together a sentence.

Damn it. I was only going to make things awkward if I didn't say something. I might cause them to worry about me.

"My last...school was...um, not like this school... Not private, I mean... One of the, uh, many public schools."

It's okay. It's okay. It's okay.

"There were...about two hundred students...in each grade."

It's already in the past.

"The class I...was in charge of..."

It's supposed to be behind me.

I couldn't get out another word.

"...? Mr. Hitoma? Oh, you must have already forgotten the details," Ms. Saotome said.

I hadn't. I couldn't. But her happy-go-lucky voice pulled me out of the mire.

"Um... Oh, ha-ha-ha! You might be right! Gosh, I feel like I can't remember anything about the past these days!"

"Heh-heh! I know what you mean! Sometimes I even forget what I ate for dinner last night!" She turned to Mr. Hoshino. "But I bet *you* never have that problem!"

"Huh? No, I forget things, too."

"Really? But you're so smart!"

"I meant to ask—have the two of you worked here the whole time?" I said.

"Yep!" Ms. Saotome replied. "I started right after I graduated!"

"I changed jobs once," Mr. Hoshino said.

Hmm? He did? Then he's…the same as me.

"Were you a teacher before?"

"Oh, well, I—"

Ms. Saotome cut in. "Mr. Hoshino is actually super amazing! He graduated top of his class at Harvard University and was a big-shot researcher!"

What?

Har…Harvard? Top of his class…?

"No, no, no! You've got it wrong!" he insisted. "Sorry, Mr. Hitoma. My background isn't anything that impressive!" He then turned to Ms. Saotome. "Ms. Yuki, I told you this already! Yes, I was first in my class, and yes, I went to college in the States, but I didn't go to Harvard!"

"Whoops, really? I'm sorry. Foreign languages aren't my forte…"

"I don't think that's the problem…" Mr. Hoshino sighed. "Anyway, to answer your question: Before this job, I was just a regular researcher. I mostly worked with genetics."

"Genetics…," I muttered.

Wait a second… Could it be…?

"Hold on—you're studying the genes of the students in this offbeat school…?!"

"No, no, no, no, no! You're mistaken! I wouldn't do something so creepy! My specialty was plants! I wanted to make delicious coffee, and that's how I got started experimenting with coffee bean genes."

"Ah… I misunderstood. My apologies."

"It's all right. Come try some more of my coffee if you'd like. If you drop by the math prep room, I'm happy to brew you a cup anytime."

"Thank you for the offer."

His coffee really was first-rate. I was delighted I'd be able to drink more of it.

"Right, then," said Mr. Hoshino. "It's about time we get to class."

A frisson of nervousness shot through me. I straightened up.

"Yes, sir...!"

This is it.

I was in charge of the advanced class and Mr. Hoshino the intermediate. Ms. Saotome wasn't assigned a homeroom.

Why was I picked over the other teachers? I wondered, of course, but apparently, that had been decided by the director of the school board. I hadn't been told anything more than that.

I picked up the student profiles. It was only a few sheets, but they felt heavy in my hand.

All right, this is where everything truly begins.

* * *

Game time.

I stood in front of the classroom door and took a deep breath.

For insurance, I skimmed over the students' backgrounds one last time. I had already reviewed the documents several times, so I should be able to match the names to the faces.

Everything will be fine.

I set my hand on the door to my new class and slid it open with purpose.

"You're doing it wrong, Tobari! You have to drop your hips lower for 'Soran Bushi'!"

"Huh? Isn't that what I'm doing?"

"Lower! 'Soran Bushi' is a Hokkaido folk song sung by fishermen when they're hauling herring! Your stance is too slack! Put your back into it! Dance is a form of physical expression. You must internalize the story behind the choreography and manifest it with your entire body. That is what it means to dance!"

What should I find but girls dancing to "Soran Bushi."

You might be wondering what in the world I'm talking about, but I, too, had no idea what was going on. I'd been told the school was free-spirited, as befitting its peculiar nature, but I never could have imagined this.

What are these girls doing first thing in the semester...?

If I remembered right...the girl with the blue hair and a passion for dance was Kyouka Minazuki, and the orange-haired one who looked like she was being held hostage was Tobari Haneda.

"Okay! One more time from the top!" Minazuki said, raring to go.

"Nope," I cut in without thinking. "It's time for homeroom."

Minazuki whipped around to look at me. She straightened up, a smile blossoming on her face.

"I'm sorry, Mr. Hitoma! I hadn't noticed you were here! It's a pleasure to make your acquaintance! My name is Kyouka Minazuki! Ah, that's right. We have homeroom now! I'll return to my seat immediately!"

She smiled elegantly and glided back to her seat.

Oh, she's more sensible than I thought.

"...It's way too early for you to be this hyper. You're ridiculously large to begin with, so you already make a racket by default," a third girl grumbled.

"Sorry, Usami. But I like the way you dance, too! Please allow me to watch you dance again!"

"N. O. No."

"Oh... So cruel..."

The disgruntled rabbit who turned away with a "Hmph!" was Sui Usami. Sitting next to her was a girl with a large tail and ears named Isaki Oogami. *She* looked mild-tempered, at least.

"Um...Mr. Hitoma? Is something wrong?" Oogami asked me.

I'd been staring at the students in a daze, bowled over by the fantasy-like scene when presented with it up close.

"Oh, sorry."

I mustn't forget this is reality.

Right, I'm on the clock.

"Saaay," Haneda drawled, leaning on the podium propped up on her elbows. "Don't tell me you're all spooked 'cause we're not human."

Her tone was probing, and her lips were curled into a smirk. My momentary anxiety hadn't gone unnoticed.

"You worked at an ordinary school for humans, right?" she added. "You said so earlier in your speech. Now that you've seen us in the flesh, I bet you're grossed out, aren't you?"

A jab to the face out of left field.

Haneda fixed me with her gaze. The warm atmosphere in the class-room frosted over. My face stiffened. For a brief moment, I fumbled for the right words to say before I realized I wasn't going to find them. Instead, I simply told her my initial reaction.

"I'm not grossed out."

"Oh yeah?"

Haneda didn't seem particularly impressed by my initial response.

I pressed on. At the moment, honesty was the best policy.

"...I admit I was surprised at first. I sat for the interview believing I was applying to teach at a so-called ordinary high school attended by humans. When the principal told me on my first day here that, 'Actually, the students here aren't human,' I couldn't believe my ears."

Up until now, I'd never met anyone with animal ears or wings or fins.

They belonged in the realm of fantasy, visions from a daydream. Sadly, I had grown up into your banal, run-of-the-mill adult and had, for better or worse, learned about the realities of life.

The world I lived in had no room for imagination.

It was packed chock-full of reality, which ate up your days as the price for merely staying alive.

This school was different.

"The classes and grade levels and everything else are different from what I'm familiar with. The curriculum itself is different. I don't know if any of my experiences will help me. Even so—"

There were countless reasons I could give for not wanting to do this. Even so, I—

"—I was happy."

"Happy?" Haneda echoed, taken aback by the unexpected response.

I hadn't expected those words to come out of my mouth, either.

Huh. I was happy.

"Yeah…that's right. Happy. Of course I was. All my life, supernatural beings had been the stuff of fiction. That had been common sense… I was happy to know humans aren't the only ones in this world. I hate humans. I don't know how to deal with them…"

It wasn't always this way, I thought but didn't say out loud.

I used to like being with other people, learning about them. I wanted to help people in any way I could. But I hadn't been able to do anything.

I had been conceited. In the end, I threw away everything and grew to hate humans.

"Tell me—I don't mean to throw you for a loop, but why do you all want to be human?" I asked. "Humans are selfish and inconsiderate of others. They use and abuse good intentions and play honest people as fools. What is there to gain from diving into a pool of sharks? Why—?"

"'Cause despite all that, we still admire them," Haneda cut in. "Say, Mr. Hitoma. Do you like humans?" she asked me knowingly, as if she could see right through me. But at the same time, her tone was tinged with sadness.

In her blue eyes glimmered a spark of expectation.

Surely, she liked humans. Me, on the other hand:

"I despise them," I said. "However..."

It wasn't as if I'd set out wanting to hate them.

Yet that was where I'd ended up. I'd suffered a wound that I still carried with me, one that had never healed.

That was all.

"Actually...that's precisely why I ran away to this place."

After hearing my answer, Haneda smiled boldly.

"Really? Sounds a bit egotistical if you ask me, but I'm more inclined to believe you for it. Oh, sorry for asking outta the blue! Thanks for telling us!"

She placed her palms together in front of her face in apology, sticking out her tongue and winking sassily. Then she sat back down at her desk. She was likely something of a leader to the class.

The tension in the air up until a moment ago eased. Somehow, I'd managed to win their approval to a degree...

I think?

"Let me introduce myself again. My name is Rei Hitoma. I'm twenty-nine years old. I teach Society and Communication. My favorite food is sushi. My hobby is video games. I play games of every genre, from new releases to retro games. Like I said during the opening ceremony, before coming here, I taught at a school for humans. I've been told that whether you can become human or not will be decided in this one year in the advanced class. If you ever have any concerns, please don't hesitate to talk to me."

I gave the same self-intro I had at the opening ceremony with a few personal details added in.

"Do you have any questions?" I asked for propriety's sake. Hardly anyone ever asked things at times like—

"I do, I do! Do you have a girlfriend?"

"Please, Haneda, don't give me grief with cookie-cutter questions. And no, I do not have a girlfriend."

"That right there is a sign that he's gonna lay his hands on a student…"

"I'm not into jailbait, Usami."

"…Usami might be out of the running, but Minazuki, on the other hand… She could be a contender."

My ears picked up that mumbled slander.

"Don't pin me for a criminal, Oogami. *No one* here is a contender."

"Wait… Did you just diss me, Isaki?" Usami demanded.

"Oh! N-no! I didn't mean it that way…!" Oogami withered under Usami's glare.

…Do they get along or not? I really can't tell.

"Anyway," I cut in, "can I ask you all to introduce yourselves? Who first…? How about we start from the hallway side? Haneda, you're up."

"'Kayyy. I'm Tobari Haneda from the avian family—a bull-headed shrike, to be exact. I'm into music. I'll listen to basically anything. I want to become a human so I can play music. I wanna try a load of different instruments. Is that good enough? I based it off your intro, Mr. Hitoma."

"Yeah, thanks."

She seems used to introducing herself before an audience…

You could generally tell if a person was a good communicator by their self-introductions.

We moved on to the next student.

"Sui Usami. Rabbit family. If I had time to waste on hobbies, I'd rather study more and become a human faster. I'm here at this school because I want to repay a human who took care of me."

Having met the bare-minimum requirements, Usami plopped back down in her seat. Her body language seemed to say, *There, satisfied?*

I see… To repay a debt. She must have good experiences with humans.

Next in line was Minazuki. With an elegant smile, she said brightly, "My name is Kyouka Minazuki! I'm a mermaid! That's why I like being by the water! It soothes me! Oh, that's right! Have you been in the hot spring, Mr. Hitoma? There's an outdoor bath on the grounds! It's supposed to be very restorative! Also, my hobby is watching dance videos! And I like music! I want to be human so I can dance! Sad to say, mermaids like me don't have legs but fins, which are not conducive to dainty and airy choreography. If I had legs—"

"You're talking too much." Usami put an end to Minazuki's rapid-fire speech. "She'll go on forever if you let her, Hitoma."

"R-right..."

Minazuki was sociable and a strong speaker. And what a wide range of interests.

"That's good, Minazuki. I'll listen to the rest another time."

I had intended to listen to the end, but unfortunately, homeroom was only so long.

"No problem! Thank you for listening!" Minazuki smiled again and sat down.

"Oh, um... I'm next...I guess...?" Last but not least was Oogami, who sat by the window. She slowly got to her feet. "Uhhh...I'm Isaki Oogami... I'm a wolf...or something."

"Or something?" I asked.

"Ah, I, uh...sometimes I turn human, maybe...or like, it's me but also not me..."

"What?"

What is she talking about?

"Eep! I, erm... I'm like a wolf...but like...a werewolf..." Her gaze flitted restlessly around the room as she spoke, as if she was admitting something she really didn't want to. "I'm here because...I want to graduate from this half-baked existence as a werewolf... That's it."

Done speaking, she sat heavily down in her seat.

It looked like she'd tried her best. Even after her introduction, she was still holding herself rigid, shaking in her seat. Maybe she was the type who got nervous in front of a crowd. I felt a little sorry for her, but at the same time, I admired her for facing something she was bad at.

Through the introductions, I was able to get a sense of everyone's personalities.

Good.

Haneda was the charismatic leader. Usami was the aloof trash-talker. Then we had the ladylike Minazuki and her sunny personality. Rounding out the group was Oogami, serious and unassuming.

Each had their reasons for wanting to become human.

These students who wanted to be human had been paired with me, a misanthrope.

"With that out of the way, here's to a good year."

I was going to teach the students about humans, about our culture and ways.

At the same time, I was going to learn from them, too.

They would teach me about the humans they admired and loved.

A **Misanthrope**
Teaches a Class for
Demi-Humans

Mr. Hitoma, Won't You Teach Us About Humans...?

The Misanthrope and the Crown of Foam

A MISANTHROPE TEACHES A CLASS FOR DEMI-HUMANS

It started on a whim.

I was born in the ocean.

In the deep, dark depths of the ocean floor.

I knew about humans.

They looked like us but were slightly different.

Instead of a tail, they had *legs*. Two of them.

Misshapen. Pitiful. Unable to swim freely through the water.

I've got an idea. Why not go see them for myself? I thought.

We weren't supposed to go near the surface. However, I, of all people, had the right to.

I wanted to see them, those creatures called humans.

That's right. In the beginning, it was just a whim.

I had a tail, but there was nowhere I could go.

I was sick of those dreary days. It was but a fleeting whim.

* * *

Sunlight streamed in through the windows of the teachers' office.

"Okay, that's everything," I mumbled. I was finishing up organizing the photos from the opening ceremony at Mr. Hoshino's request.

The students' appearances had surprised me at first, but I gradually got used to it. Maybe that was proof that I was assimilating.

"Ah, Mr. Hitoma, good morning!"

An angel appeared in the middle of the teachers' office.

"Ms. S-Saotome! Good morning!"

Ms. Saotome had been my oasis since I first arrived, and that day, she was just as lovely as always.

"Have you gotten used to working here?" she asked. "You're coming up on three weeks now; is that right?"

"Yes, I have, thanks to everyone's support. I seem to be picking things up."

I let out a stiff laugh. I was happy to get the chance to talk with her, but speaking with beautiful women always had me tongue-tied.

She laughed softly. "Ha-ha. That's good to hear!" Her guileless smile was like a soothing balm.

The door to the teachers' office opened again.

"Ah. Mr. Hitoma. You're here early. Morning."

Mr. Hoshino ambled over toward me, his back hunched. He smelled faintly of coffee.

Did he brew a cup in the math prep room before coming over?

"Good morning, Mr. Hoshino."

"It's been a few weeks since you started. How is everything? Used to it yet?"

"Wow! I asked him the same thing a second ago!!" Ms. Saotome exclaimed. "He said it's working out!"

"That so? Happy to hear it."

"Yes, and thank you both for your help."

"Don't mention it. As long as you're finding everything all right." Mr. Hoshino nodded with a slight smile before returning to his own desk, which was buried under piles of documents, and getting to work.

...I haven't paid much attention to it before, but the things on his desk seem to multiply every time I look at it.

I was sincerely grateful toward them. It was a big help that they'd made

the time to chat with me. No doubt this kind of small talk was an important part of establishing healthy communication.

Small talk, huh… Not my area of expertise per se…

But I'll give it a shot. Next time, I'll try chitchatting with my students.

* * *

"Random question, but what are the dorms here like?"

It was at the end of fourth period, which for me was history, the last
class of the morning. As soon as it was over, I made an attempt to converse
with Usami sitting right in front of me.

"What do you mean, what are they like? I don't understand what you
want to know," she said, her words incisive.

A fastball down the middle…!

"Oh, sorry, sorry. Um, I heard you all have private rooms, but the
bathrooms and cafeteria are shared? I was just wondering how you like
living there."

"Don't pry into my private life."

She threw me a cold stare before turning away.

Maybe I picked the wrong person to attempt small talk with.

"Hmm? Are you eating lunch in the classroom today, Mr. Hitoma?"
Minazuki asked me cheerfully as I wilted where I was standing. "Would
you like to eat together, then?"

She must have been trying to cheer me up…

"Thank you, Minazuki. I hadn't planned to eat here, but you're right.
It's a good opportunity. I'll stay. Let me drop by the teachers' office to pick
up my lunch."

"Kyouka! I see you trying to butter him up! No fair!"

Usami was pouting even though a second ago she was the one who had
been so frosty. Maybe she was thinking that Minazuki was trying to get a
jump on the teacher evaluations.

"Well! Why don't you join us, then?"

"No way!"

Haneda saw us bickering and walked over with a grin. "Ooh, what's this? You guys fighting over Mr. Hitoma?"

"Exactly, Tobari. Winner takes all."

"Winner takes all?!" I blurted out, parroting Minazuki's words without thinking.

They're fighting over me...

Sure, they were students, but I never thought I'd see the day... I knew nothing could happen given our respective positions, but I didn't hate having girls vie for my attention. I felt like the protagonist in a romantic comedy. It was kind of nice...

"Wipe that grin off your face, Hitoma. Don't misunderstand. We're not fighting over *you*. We're fighting over our grades."

I'd been smiling despite myself, and Usami gave me a verbal lashing for my carelessness.

"Th-there's no misunderstanding," I said.

"That so? Whatever."

Misunderstanding? What misunderstanding? I'm not crying or anything...

Minazuki clapped her hands together in front of her chest. "So be it! Today, we'll all eat together! How's that?"

"Sure, whatever," Usami said.

"Fine by me!" Haneda added.

"Then it's settled!" Minazuki turned to Oogami, who was sitting alone at her desk by the window, laying out her lunch. "Isaki! You'll eat with us, too, right?"

Oogami's ears and tail twitched, and she stole a peek at me. Our eyes met, but she looked away immediately.

She gave the invitation a moment's thought and said, "Ah, um... if you're okay with me joining, then..." She dipped her head in a small bow.

I had to go back to the teachers' office to fetch my lunch, so I told them to start eating without me. In the office, I took a plastic bag out from the fridge. I put the ready-to-eat meal I had bought from a convenience store into the microwave and pressed the START button.

I'm gonna get sick of eating packaged food soon...

I wonder if the students make their own lunches. Oh, maybe the dorm mom makes them. Man, I want to eat food someone else cooked for me, too. Ideally, I'd really like to eat my girlfriend's cooking… If only I had a girlfriend…

As the mouthwatering scent of my microwave lunch grew stronger, so, too, did my feelings of wretchedness.

How to describe this phenomenon? It was like the fragrance was shoving in my face how alone I was…

I was busy staring down reality when my lunch finished heating. I said my hellos and good-byes to the other teachers and headed back to the classroom.

Right at that moment…

"Eeeeyaaaaah!!!!!"

A shriek split the air. That sounded like Minazuki's voice. *What happened?*

I ran back to class.

"What's wrong?! What's going on?! Is everyone okay?!" I shouted, louder than I meant to. The students all jumped in surprise.

Usami glared at me. "Shut it! Kyouka is fine! *You're* the one who's making a racket!"

"Oh, sorry…"

"Don't say that! I started it by shouting! It was my fault in the first place!" Minazuki insisted. She was the one who'd screamed. "Don't worry, Mr. Hitoma! Thank you for your concern…!"

Her face was pale, but she didn't seem to be injured.

I relaxed slightly. "Um… So what is it?"

"N-nothing important. It's just…there was a mix-up with the lunches the dorm mom prepared for me…," she said hesitantly with a pained expression, her gaze averted from the lunch in question.

Her lunch? Did a bug end up inside?

I looked at the spread she had out in front of her.

…It appeared to be a perfectly ordinary packed lunch. It reminded me in some way of the lunches my mom used to make for me. Rice, sides, and a salad. The standard menu.

"Kyouka can't eat fish cakes," Haneda explained.

I must've looked confused.

"Ugh…I'm so embarrassed…" Minazuki buried her face in her hands.

Fish cakes…?

"…You see, I'm a mermaid, so I can't really partake in the so-called bounties of the sea. In order to become human, I've managed to get to the point where I can just barely stand to look at grilled fish and sashimi! But…I can't…I just *can't* stand fish cakes. I can't help thinking how cruel they are…!"

I see. That's why she screamed.

I checked the contents of her lunch again.

Here's the problem.

Inside were a few slices of fish cake with a cute character design.

Kyouka Minazuki.

Mermaid. Enrolled three years ago. Promoted to the advanced class this year. Wants to be human so that she can dance.

"*Hic…* What do I do…? She went to all this trouble of making me lunch. I would feel bad if I didn't finish it…"

Minazuki kept her face turned away from her food so the fish cakes didn't enter her line of sight.

Got it. I'll—

"Hey, Kyouka, how about we switch?"

Beaten to the punch…

Minazuki beamed at Oogami's suggestion. "Yay! Are you sure?! You're my savior, Isaki! I don't know how to thank you! By the way, are there any foods you don't like to eat?"

"Not particularly. I'll be taking your fish cakes, then." To put Minazuki at ease, Oogami opened her mouth wide and stuffed her face with the fish cakes. "Ahhh-mmmm!" She munched on the slices and swallowed them. "All finished! They're gone, Kyouka…!"

"Thank you! I can always count on you! You're my hero!"

Minazuki was raving over Oogami, and I found myself a *tiny* bit envious.

…If I had eaten her fish cakes, would she have lavished me with praise, too?

"Hmmmm, I had your fish cakes, so in return— Oh, do you want my rolled omelet?" Oogami asked.

"I couldn't! That's too much!"

"It's all right. Take it."

I had thought of Oogami as a reserved student who didn't like to stand out, but apparently, she was actually quite nurturing.

The two of them made a good pair.

Now that the problem is resolved, I might as well drink some tea…

Having negotiated the exchange, Oogami picked up her rolled omelet with her chopsticks and held it out to Minazuki.

"Here, Kyouka, say *aah*."

"Ugck—!!"

I nearly spat out my tea, unable to believe what was transpiring in front of me.

Say aah*?! This is a real phenomenon?! It's never happened once to me in my twenty-nine years of life!*

Is this normal in the world of high school girls?! Is it?!

"Oh my, thank you!" Minazuki closed her lips around Oogami's chopsticks with a smile. Her delighted expression seemed to say, *Yummy!*

What should I do? I feel like I shouldn't be here…

"…You're gawking, Mr. Hitoma," Haneda teased. She was watching me with a smirk playing on her lips.

"N-no! I'm not!"

"Disgusting," Usami sneered.

I panicked. "Y-you've got the wrong idea, both of you!"

The two of them rolled their eyes at me.

Minazuki and Oogami continued enjoying their lunches.

* * *

I had fifth period free. I planned to use it to prep for the intermediate class I was teaching sixth period, so I left the classroom.

As I was leaving, Haneda poked her head out the door and called to me.

"Mr. Hitoma, you free next period?"

"Not exactly, but what is it?"

This was an inquiry from Haneda, who took pleasure in ribbing me. I had a feeling she wasn't about to say something pleasant. She could even be planning something downright wicked.

"You seeee, we have gym next. Won't you come observe?"

"Observe your gym class?"

"Yep. It's the quickest way for you to understand our strengths and weaknesses, I think."

"Okay... I guess?"

For the purposes of the students' evaluations, it was important to have a grasp of how similar their physical capabilities were to a human's. I guess that's why observing PE class was a good idea.

For example, students in the beginner class who weren't used to their bodies were known to walk on all fours when their attention slipped.

Needless to say, they were docked points for diverging from human behavior.

"Who's the gym teacher?" I asked Haneda.

"Ms. Sudou. I already got her permission."

"Um, way to put the cart before the horse..."

She asked Ms. Sudou before checking in with me?

"Hey, it's important to be proactive," she said nonchalantly.

But how many people out there actually act on their thoughts?

I could see why Haneda belonged in the advanced class.

Proactive...that's the exact opposite of me...

I caved.

"Fine... It's a good opportunity. Why not...?"

"Sweet. Thanks." She turned back to the others. "Hey! Mr. Hitoma says he's gonna come watch gym class!"

Minazuki came bounding out of the room, her eyes sparkling.

"Mr. Hitoma! Are you really coming to observe us?! How exciting! We're going to be dancing today! Everyone's spectacular! I'd love for you to come see!"

Ah, they're having dance class. Minazuki said she wanted to dance, didn't she? Today's class is right up her alley, then.

"Oh no... Mr. Hitoma's going to be watching," said Oogami. "I'm starting to get a little nervous..."

"Forget about him. Think of him as furniture. That's all he is anyway."

Usami... She seemed to think of me as so much dirt on her shoe, but at least her compassion for Oogami was admirable.

"Usamiii...," Oogami whimpered.

"Stop sniffling. It's getting on my nerves."

Apparently, I wasn't the only target of Usami's sharp tongue. She was that way toward everyone.

* * *

Gym class.

At this school, the purpose of the class wasn't to evaluate students through competitions of strength and stamina but to teach them the intricate ways humans moved. Dance was one of the activities in the curriculum. The goal was to have students learn about humans' subtler, more subdued gestures.

The gymnasium was connected to the main building, where the teachers' office and classrooms were located, by a passageway.

It was about as large as two full-size basketball courts, pretty big considering the small student body.

The door rattled as I slid it open, and I stepped inside. The sight of the somewhat dusty hall filled me with nostalgia.

The students had already changed into exercise clothing and were sitting on the floor with their arms wrapped around their knees in front of them.

The gym teacher, Ms. Sudou, was there as well. I had heard that she had once competed in nationals for swimming. She was tall, slim, and had a gorgeous figure. Her long black hair was tied up in a bun that day.

"Great! The gang's all here! Let's get started!" Her clear voice echoed through the gymnasium. She spotted me standing by the entrance, and our eyes met. "Ah, Mr. Hitoma. Good to have you with us today."

She executed a perfect, textbook bow.

On the other hand, thrown off rhythm as I was, my bow was clumsy. "Sorry to spring this on you," I said. "I'm happy to be here."

My socially awkward self had no idea what to do in these kinds of situations. It might've been just my personal bias, but gym teachers seemed so self-assured, like they seized life by the horns and always put their best foot forward. The way they shone made the shadow I lived under even darker.

Oblivious to my inferiority complex, Ms. Sudou told me kindly, "Just say the word if you need anything," before turning back to the students.

"All right. Today, we're picking up where we left off last dance class. First, I want to see what you learned last time. We'll go in order of your student IDs. Usami, you're up first."

"Fine," Usami said curtly and walked to the front.

The other students sat by the wall, their knees propped up. I decided to position myself nearby and watch, too. I was already here, anyway.

Usami took her place. A sweet, upbeat pop song with an electronic backing track started playing from the portable speaker next to Ms. Sudou. I guessed it was her assigned song.

So cute.

Usami leaped, hopped, and twirled lightly on her feet. Her movements were airy and buoyant, but her steps were sure. The style was similar to ballet. She kept a cool expression even during difficult portions, executing the moves like they were no big deal.

Some of the choreography was cutesy and sweet. I wondered if that was what Usami was into. She looked so surly throughout the entire dance; she didn't smile even once. Nevertheless, you could say that the performance was all the more Usami for it.

I felt like I was at a live show for an idol. Not that I'd ever been to one. However, she reminded me of the girls who popped up on my social media feeds once in a while. She clearly understood what her own charms were. The dance was on the cute side and demonstrated her personal strengths.

The song ended, and Usami struck a final pose.

What a performance—

"Usami!!!! You. Were. WONDERFUL!!!!"

A burst of applause rang out through the gym courtesy of an overexcited Minazuki.

"Gah?!"

It wasn't just your normal clapping, either, but a standing ovation at that.

"You're hurting my ears!"

"Usami! I'm obsessed with those adorable, dainty moves! Seeing you dance fills me with joy!" Minazuki exclaimed, shoving herself so close to Usami that it looked like they were going to collide. "You added a new bit of choreo in the middle, right? *Sigh...* I could learn a thing or two from your sense of rhythm... Please teach me later!"

"Personal space! Stop blabbering already and sit down!"

"Oh dear, I'm sorry. Silly me."

Minazuki returned to her seat.

Ms. Sudou finished scribbling on an evaluation form and looked up, capping off Minazuki and Usami's tiff. "That was great, Usami. Very authentic."

"Anything I can improve?"

To be able to ask for feedback without a moment's delay... Her initiative was admirable. I was genuinely impressed.

"Hmm, let me think... Your song is 'A Dream within a Wonderland,' right? The dance fits the music, so I don't have any comments on that front. If I had to give any advice, it would be to smile. Intentionally keeping your expression stoic is certainly an option, but didn't you say last class that you wanted to bring out a fun mood? In that case—and I'm sorry to tell you the same thing every time—all that's left for you to work on is your smile."

"...Got it," Usami said, seemingly dissatisfied.

Come to think of it, I've never seen Usami smile. She was hungry for a good evaluation and worked hard for it, but smiling wasn't her forte. That could have been the reason her ears were drooping.

"Oogami, you're up next!" Ms. Sudou called.

"R-right!"

Oogami went up on shaky legs and took her position. Unlike Usami, she seemed insecure and uncomfortable presenting in front of a crowd.

A different song played from the speaker. It was a cool, acoustic tune. Oogami began dancing.

...It's kind of...seductive.

Her movements were surprisingly lithe and dynamic. She must've been playing to her strength and stamina. How unexpected.

When the song ended, Minazuki gave another loud round of applause. She looked like she was really enjoying herself. And yet, she kept glancing around her and fidgeting. I wondered why.

Oh, it must be because Usami is glaring at her.

Haneda watched over the scene with amusement.

"Haneda is next."

"Okaaay," Haneda drawled and stepped forward, exuding confidence as she stood before her audience.

Lively rock music reverberated through the room.

Her performance was meticulous and clean.

Gone was her usual cheeky and lofty attitude. I was reminded that she was an accomplished student. She didn't make any mistakes. On all the quizzes I'd given so far, she'd never gotten anything less than a full score. You could tell through her dance that she was the type to do everything she could properly.

Things came effortlessly to her. That was precisely why she could perfect every single detail, down to the expression on her face.

...The year's no-doubt leading candidate for graduation was in a league of her own.

The song ended with a final *da-dum!* Haneda topped off her performance with a glowing smile.

Minazuki applauded loudly. Oogami clapped as well but softly. Usami glowered at Haneda with frustration.

"Perfect. I have nothing to add," Ms. Sudou said.

"Cheers," Haneda replied lazily before returning to join the other three.

Where had her passion a minute ago disappeared to?

Unable to help herself, Minazuki burst out, "Haneda! You're amazing! Everything was impeccable, from the tips of your fingers down to your toes! Your dance was super-duper cool!!!!!!"

That earned her another glare from Usami, but she just had to share her excitement with Haneda.

"Ah-ha-ha, thanks!"

"Kyouka! You're next. Hurry up and show us your dance," Usami said, pushing Minazuki forward.

"All right! Will do!"

She was trembling with enthusiasm. It was obvious from looking at her how much she loved dancing.

"Are you ready, Minazuki?" Ms. Sudou asked.

"Yes, I am!"

Must be nice being so full of life. Her radiance was blinding for someone like me.

The music started. *Is this jazz?* It was an upbeat, acoustic track. Minazuki started to dance.

...I get it now.

Errr, yeah, I see.

To put it one way, her dancing was *quirky*. It most closely resembled the kind of spirited folk dance that I'd walked in on the day of the opening ceremony.

I would be hard-pressed to call her *good*, even out of politeness. She was off-beat and awkward. Her steps were faltering. I was breaking out in a cold sweat, worried that she was going to trip.

However, she looked like she was having more fun than anyone else had. The choreography was a bloated, mismatched amalgamation of moves she wanted to try out. She made a ruckus when she fumbled a somersault. And yet, her expression proclaimed her joy for the world to see.

Her performance conveyed that dancing was meant to be fun.

When the song ended, she bowed and panted, "Thank you for watching!"

Haneda and Oogami clapped, and I found myself clapping along with them.

"Thanks, Minazuki. It was fun for us in the audience, too," Ms. Sudou commented. "Hmm. If you pay more attention to the rhythm and movements, I'm sure you'll improve!"

"Thank you for the feedback! Will do! I'll pay more attention!" Minazuki's smile was like a burst of sunlight.

Usami watched her dispassionately.

* * *

The incident happened toward the end of class, when I was idly watching the students practice.

"…Hn?" Ms. Sudou made a surprised sound.

"What's wrong, Ms. Sudou?"

"Oh, Haneda. It's nothing really. The speaker is on the fritz…"

I overheard their conversation and walked up to take a peek out of curiosity.

Once in a while, the track playing from the portable speaker by Ms. Sudou skipped.

"Oh boy. Are we gonna manage?" Haneda asked.

"Hmm, I'll go bring a backup just in case…," Ms. Sudou said.

"Ah, I can go."

I raised my hand, listening in next to them. In this scenario, as a mere observer, I was undoubtedly the best candidate for errand boy.

"Thanks, Mr. Hitoma. But do you know where to go? The speakers are kept in the PE prep room."

Oof...

I didn't know where that was. My hand drooped from where it was hanging in the air.

"It's okay. Don't worry about it, Mr. Hitoma. You've just started here! I'll pop over and be back in a jiff. Can you look after the students in the meantime?"

My offer had backfired. I ended up imposing on Ms. Sudou's kindness...

"Uh, all right," I replied.

"Thank you. I'll just be a second."

She then left the gymnasium to fetch the speaker.

"Objects are destined to break, I guess...," Haneda said, holding the malfunctioning speaker. She stated the seemingly obvious truth with earnestness.

"Yeah. The individual parts wear down with use," I replied.

The speaker in question looked like an older model. It must have broken down over the years, hence the hiccupping sound.

"This speaker must be reaching the end of its life span," Haneda said to me.

"Maybe so. Sometimes you have to replace audio equipment like earphones as quickly as in a year."

"Hmm."

...That's right. Haneda said she was interested in music. What does she normally use to listen to it? Maybe she's in the camp that doesn't often use speakers. This is a good opportunity. Let me try talking to her about music.

"Haneda—"

"Cut it out! Stop nagging me when you suck, too!"

The sudden outburst rang out through the gym, silencing everyone else.

I looked around for the instigator.

It was Usami.

At the other end of her gaze was Minazuki, who was wide-eyed with shock at being yelled at. Minazuki took a breath before smiling gently at Usami.

"I'm sorry, Usami. I was being too pushy."

"That grin on your face pisses me off," Usami snapped. "You're *weird*. You say you like to dance, but you're awful at it, and you've got no talent. It doesn't matter if you become human or not. You're not gonna be able to dance anyway—"

"Hold on, Usami, that's going too far," I hurried to interrupt. She'd clearly crossed the line.

"It's true, though. Are you gonna baby her forever? If liking something was all it took, no one would ever need to make an effort!"

"Usami," I cautioned again.

Minazuki's smile didn't waver under the assault of Usami's dream-crushing tirade.

"It's quite all right, Mr. Hitoma. I don't disagree with her on this point. I know better than anyone that I'm the worst dancer of the group."

She was wearing her usual elegant smile, but that and her tone, sad to say, seemed forced.

"However, I am confident that my love of dance is greater than anyone else's. I'm betting my entire life to be here. I will show you that love is enough. Love is a weapon. That's what I believe, and that belief has carried me all the way to where I am now."

Hers was the declaration of someone who had faith she could do anything.

By her logic, people who couldn't turn love into success only lacked willpower, lacked drive.

And me, back then—had I been lacking something, too?

"I can't stand that attitude of yours. The fact that you can be so blasé about your own failure just means you've given up. You're just putting on a front, and it makes you look like a fool."

"So you say... However, my appetite for learning simply outweighs any frustration."

"You're full of hot air. Don't you feel any shame? Or are you just being condescending to the rest of us?"

"No, I'm not!" Minazuki refuted loudly, grabbing Usami's hands tightly. Gone was her mellow demeanor from a second ago. "I'm not looking down at you! I think you're amazing! The way you throw your entire self into your dance stole my breath away! I respect the way you always hold yourself to such high standards and aim for perfection and try to improve yourself! I feel blessed to be able to study alongside you to become human, and I learn from you all the time! You're absolutely wonderful, Usami!"

The wave of compliments from the earnest Minazuki crashed into Usami dead-on.

"Sh-sh-sh-sh-shut up!" She blushed all the way to the tips of her rabbit ears.

Minazuki chuckled. "Yes, I do tend to go on at times."

The tension eased up a little.

There were ten more minutes left in class. Ms. Sudou came rushing back into the gym. She signaled the students to gather so they could perform again before the class ended.

* * *

I thanked Ms. Sudou for letting me observe and returned to the teachers' office to prepare for my next lesson.

Observing the PE class had taught me that Oogami was surprisingly the most athletic, followed by Haneda, then Usami, with Minazuki coming in last. Also, that Minazuki and Usami mixed as well as oil and water...

I left the teachers' office for my sixth-period intermediate class, my mind still occupied with worries.

I wonder if Minazuki's all right. Usami said a lot of awful things to her...

On my way there, I spotted the person herself. Speak of the devil.

"Ah, Minazuki," I called out to her without thinking.

"Hi!"

Minazuki had changed out of her gym clothes and was back in her usual black dress.

What should I say…? I'll only make her uncomfortable if I'm too forward…

"Um, uhhh, your dance—it was good."

Booooring. Is that the best I can do…?

"Oh my! I'm delighted! Thank you very much!"

Minazuki's smile was radiant despite how lackluster and generic my praise had been.

Come to think of it, I'd only ever seen positive emotions on her face.

"…Amazing," I mumbled.

"What?"

Oh, whoops. Didn't mean to say that out loud.

I tried to cover my slipup.

"Um, I meant that earlier Usami, you know, said a lot of hurtful things to you. I think it's amazing how well you took it."

Another fumbled response!

Wait, maybe I should stop blathering on about this incident already! I might have stuck my foot in my mouth again! I meant to make her feel better, but I think I just threw salt in her wound! Did I mess up? I…

As I stood haplessly with my thoughts swirling in my head, Minazuki smiled at me softly.

"…You're kind, Mr. Hitoma." She sounded happy. "No matter what anyone says, all I want is to remain the 'me' I like, always. That is what my pride is for!" she boasted with her hand on her chest. "You know, there's a saying that I'm fond of! 'Tomorrow is another day'!"

Where do I remember that from?

There's a book I read a long time ago, back in college. It was called—

"*Gone with the Wind*, right?"

Minazuki clapped her hands together, beaming sunnily. "Exactly! I read it for class soon after enrolling! It's embarrassing to admit, but at that time, I couldn't do anything right. I was a mess. I had no space in my heart for anything, and I lost sight of myself, the me I like."

As she recalled her past, her gaze was focused on somewhere far away. "I hated myself back then," she said.

Even Minazuki went through something like that.

She's the same as me.

"I was overwhelmed." Minazuki smiled sadly. "My upbringing was strict, and my entire future had already been laid out... That's why my parents refused to allow me to enroll at first."

"You mean...um...you're the heiress of a well-to-do family? Like your family has a long and noble history or something like that?"

Minazuki reacted to my bumbling response with a blank stare. Then she giggled.

"Have you heard of Poseidon, Mr. Hitoma? He was a warden of the ocean."

"Huh? Oh, I have. Through games. He's one of those gods from the myths, right? Shirtless, rugged-looking fella, carries a trident?"

"Ha-ha! That shirtless, rugged-looking fella is my ancestor."

"You're talking about one of the A-tier gods!!"

He actually existed?! Does that mean Minazuki is descended from a god...?

"Before he passed, he left the supervision of the oceans to his children. His children, his grandchildren, and everyone after have protected the seas for generations as wardens. At times, wardens must exercise the privileges of their station to change the currents and regulate the planet's temperature and climate or to intervene with the lives of the ocean inhabitants."

What I was hearing was outrageous.

If what she was saying was true, didn't these wardens basically hold power over the entire world?

"Originally, the one who was supposed to inherit the vast expanse of the seas was me! I'm a direct descendant of Poseidon and an only child, so I was at the head of the line for succession rights. Given my position, my parents were deeply opposed to me attending this school."

I'll bet...

I'd thought Minazuki gave off the air of a well-to-do young lady, but apparently, she wasn't from just any family.

To say her family had a long history was an understatement. It wouldn't be inaccurate to call them royalty who ruled over practically the whole world. By all rights, she wasn't someone I should be able to chat with so casually the way we were doing now.

Yet, Minazuki was here, at this school, standing right in front of me.

"But I wanted to be human…! One fateful day, I saw a human dancing on a boat. The image was burned into me! It was only once, but once was enough to transform my life."

Minazuki was gazing somewhere far off.

Perhaps that dance in her memories was even now playing through her head.

She shut her eyes slowly. Then she opened them again and looked straight at me.

"I was enraptured."

Her gaze never wavered. It was steady and earnest.

"The dancer mesmerized everyone with her delicate steps, and the mermaid that I am, she mesmerized me, too! In that moment, my dull, restricted life burst into vibrant color…! That was the first and only time I've ever felt that way! At that moment, I found my reason to live! It was like a punch to the face! I'm not exaggerating! Ahhh! That dance that embodied the flame of life, how I want to show it to the world…!"

Here was Minazuki's true self.

The soft, warm Minazuki was a facade. She was, in a word, a fanatic. That was the description I could find.

"As I said earlier, I am prepared to throw away this life of mine if I cannot become human."

"You…" I wanted to argue, but I couldn't find the right words for the situation.

Minazuki's passion was pure—but dangerous, like a highly potent poison.

"Or rather, that is the rule," Minazuki said.

"Rule?"

"Yes, rule. My parents were strongly against my wishes to become human. You see, a rule has existed since long ago that condemns mermaids who try but fail to become human within a set time frame to turn into sea-foam. It is designed to protect other mermaids, to protect our home. It is a vital precept that safeguards our race."

Minazuki was cool as a cucumber.

"What...?"

No way.

Everyone knew the fairy tale.

"...How long do you have?" I asked.

She softly held up her index finger in front of my lips like she had seen the question coming.

"I can't say. That's the rule," she answered, looking wise beyond her years.

Then she broke into a bold smile. She took a step away from me and twirled around.

"Don't worry about me, Mr. Hitoma! I will definitely become human! Even if the worst should come to pass, this is my greatest ambition. I want to remain the me I love, always!"

She threw me a charming wink.

My worries and anxieties, I was sure she understood them all. And born from her acceptance was the smile on her face.

"'Tomorrow is another day'! A fresh start! That's why I'll live today to the fullest! During my time here, I'm going to fall more and more in love with everything humans create, including dance, of course! Not just like—*love*! And so—Mr. Hitoma, please watch me from the front row! Promise me you will! No more tail for me! I want to stand firmly on two legs in this world, just like humans do!"

The ringing proclamation must have been pulled straight from her extraordinary resolve. She was standing in this place, in this moment, literally fighting for her life.

"...You're tough."

"Legs planted, chest out!" she huffed, her face glowing with pride.

Her happy-go-lucky expression was completely at odds with her mood only a second ago. I found the corners of my lips tilting upward in amusement.

Even without her classmates and me, no doubt Minazuki would be able to keep moving forward all on her own.

She was completely different from me. I couldn't do anything without other people's help.

There's no way of knowing what the future holds, but maybe by this time next year, she'll be gone from this school.

I had a feeling that was exactly what would happen.

"I expect an invitation when you take the stage as a dancer," I told her.

"You can bet on it!"

I wanted to talk with Minazuki a little longer, but the bell rang to signal the start of sixth period.

"Oh, shoot. I'm sorry, Mr. Hitoma. I have to run. I'm glad we had a chance to talk!"

"Yeah! Sorry to keep you. If your teacher gives you a hard time, tell them I held you up."

It was nothing but the truth, after all.

"I appreciate your consideration! In that case, if it looks like I'm going to get scolded, I won't hesitate to give your name!"

She stuck out her tongue like a cheeky brat.

Didn't realize she could pull a face like that.

I headed toward my next class.

Tomorrow is another day. So it is.

Maybe I'm due to give Gone with the Wind *a reread.*

A **Misanthrope**
Teaches a Class for
Demi-Humans

Mr. Hitoma, Won't You Teach Us About Humans...?

The Misanthrope and the Lonely Castle on a Full Moon's Night

A MISANTHROPE TEACHES A CLASS FOR DEMI-HUMANS

The day the full moon rises has come around once again this month.
The day I become not myself.
I am to blame for everything. *Everything.*
Me, the one whom I loathe.

* * *

Ugh… It's already the end of May…

I was looking at the calendar in the classroom and lamenting the passage of time after the end-of-the-period bell rang.

Oh, man… Since I had the beginner class first period, it's still early in the morning, and I'm already beat.

A lot of students in the beginner class weren't completely used to being demi-humans and couldn't suppress their bestial instincts, so it was common for commotions to break out in the middle of class.

The instigators were liable to be docked points for "on-campus unhuman-like behavior."

Points were deducted so often in the beginner class that, at first, I thought I was at fault for not being able to control the students. However, according to Ms. Saotome and Mr. Hoshino, "The beginner class is like kindergarten or the lower elementary school grades. Don't worry about it if things get rowdy or if you have to mark the students down a lot."

Thanks to their advice, now when the students acted out, I was able to correct their behavior and target the root causes of the point deductions. It was tiring, but you could say that I was growing.

Second period is the advanced class... They'll be a treat after dealing with the beginners.

They all listened to my lectures seriously, and the class atmosphere was usually decently calm, and—

"Ha-ha-ha! Listen, listen, don't you think *papaya* sounds kind of dirty? It's seriously hilarious!!"

Perfect example. I never have to worry about this kind of vulgar talk...

"It's in my lunch today!! Can you believe it?! Pa—pa—ya! ♥ Bwa-ha-ha-ha!! Omigod, and it's mad tasty!! For reals!!"

...with the advanced class.

Wait, wait, wait. You can't be serious.

Usami was fastidious, and Oogami would never yell so loudly—she had been absent during homeroom anyway. Minazuki didn't banter like this, either. Haneda was the most likely candidate...but she wasn't usually *this* spunky.

Did a student from another class come to hang out?

Curious, I stopped by the advanced class on the way back to the teachers' office.

I opened the door to find an unfamiliar female student with a thick cloud of brown hair and flashy clothing sitting on a desk and laughing with Minazuki and Haneda.

One of those bad-girl types...

"Oh, hey, Mr. Hitoma!" As I stood on the threshold of the classroom, the student pointed at me and laughed. "Ha-ha-ha! Now that I'm getting a good eyeful, you look like a zombie! That's *no bueno*! Hold up—is that bedhead? Actually, is that, like, on purpose? There was a time when the just-laid look was the trend for men's hairdos, right? Is that still a thing? Wait, before that, you should wear a nicer suit! Oh, but your tie's totes adorbs! Wait a sec, are you even sleeping properly? Oh, up close, your skin's looking pretty rough, too! Is that skin or parchment? Do you live in a desert? Um, big yikes! Aren't you almost thirty? You're not young anymore. You gotta get on a skincare regimen, for real!"

Slow down there!

Her rapid-fire speech was too fast. I vaguely felt insulted, but I hadn't actually absorbed any of what she'd said.

"Also, what brand of toner do you use? Hold up, do you even know what toner is?"

"Huh? Oh, uh…kind of…?"

Toner's that stuff I put on a bit of in the mornings after I shave my face. My skin's sensitive, so electric razors really do a number on me… Wait, no, that's not relevant right now. Who in the world is this glitzy, cheeky girl in front of me acting like she's my best friend?!

"'Kind of'? Ha-ha! Bet whatever you're using is trash!" she practically shouted at me. Her expression was constantly changing. "If you don't give a hoot about brands, shall I—the one, the only Isaki—tell you my favorite? I used it this morning, and let me tell you, my makeup's not budging an inch! It's the bomb! I'm in love! I seriously can't recommend anything other than hyaluronic acid. Um, hmm, I was gonna convert all of y'all today, so I'm pretty sure I put it in my makeup pouch…"

She started digging through her makeup pouch, a must-have item for a teen rebel.

Hold on. Isaki? She said "Isaki"…

"…Isaki?"

"Hmm? We're on a first-name basis now? Besties! LOL!"

I wasn't close enough to any of the students to call them by their first name. I had only voiced my thoughts out loud. Besides that—

"You're Oogami?"

She was completely different from the docile, unassuming student I knew.

"*Excuse* me? Isn't that what I just said? Oh, don't tell me you didn't notice, since this is the first time you're seeing me like this?! Ha-ha-ha! But I totes get it! For real, how would you know? Wait, didn't the principal tell you? Oh, but like, sure, I glammed up my outfit, but my fluffy hair and adorable ears are the same as always, right? And the way you're always looking at me—which is, by the way, *me-ow*—I hoped a teensy bit you'd notice, you know? Ah, I guess *bow-wow* fits me more than *meow*?"

She looked at me with a wide grin, cunningly using her cuteness to her advantage.

But she was right. Now that she mentioned it, her tail and ears were the same as Oogami's. Her style was flashier, but the actual clothing she was wearing was familiar. The usual Oogami was the dictionary definition of a model student. Her blazer was always wrinkle-free, her blouse buttoned all the way to her collar, and her skirt falling below her knees. She wore glasses and kept her hair in a neat braid.

Meanwhile, this Isaki wore her blazer hanging open and her blouse unbuttoned dangerously low. Her skirt barely covered her rear, and her hair was styled in waves, hanging loose down her back. The glasses were nowhere to be seen, either.

"Are you that mesmerized by me, Mr. Hitoma?"

Crap. I didn't mean to stare.

"Ah, no, you just look really different…"

I averted my gaze instinctively, but she stepped in front of me again, a smug smile on her face.

"Hee-hee! Cute as a button, right?! The 'normal' Isaki's a bit shy, so you might not have noticed, but I've got a pretty face and killer figure to boot!"

The transformed Oogami declared and showed off said physique by striking a pose straight out of a magazine centerfold.

Uh, erm, her cleavage… Gah… I don't know where to look.

"Ah, um, okay, I get it, Oogami. I get it already."

I again averted my eyes from the saucy girl standing before me.

"Huh? Awww, you're blushing, Mr. Hitoma! Wa-ha-ha! You're too funny!"

Oogami pointed at me as she cracked up. She seemed to be enjoying herself.

Argh… She's toying with my feelings…!

"Your heart's racing 'cause I'm so adorable. I get it. Yep! You're a man after all!" She patted me on the shoulder.

It made me the tiiiiiiniest bit happy, and I was ashamed of myself for it… Enough said about the visual stimulation.

I instinctively felt that she meant no harm. It was like when a relative's kid took a liking to you…

Besides that, there was something that had been bothering me the whole time.

"Oogami."

"Hmm? What's up?"

"Why did you change your…personality—is that it?—all of a sudden? Did anything happen?"

She's basically a wolf in sheep's clothing…I guess?

Oogami stared blankly at me, but then she grinned from ear to ear.

"What to do, what to do?" she said in a singsong voice. "Should I tell you? Should I not?"

"Oh, that's how you're going to be. It's too much of a hassle. Never mind."

Tired of being jerked around, I was about to give up on the subject entirely, but Oogami stopped me in a panic.

"Whaaaaat?! No, wait! My bad, Mr. Hitoma! I just figured the principal or one of the other teachers already told you! Wait, don't we *totally* sound like a married couple right now? I'm cracking up. Bwa-ha-ha!"

Talking to this version of Oogami sort of makes me uncomfortable…

"You see, I'm a werewolf. Didn't I say that right at the start? Basically, on the day of the full moon and only on that day, I become the me you see now. I have what you call a split personality! That brings us to today! Full-moon day! It's the first time in a while *I* get to come to school! And now you know!"

A split personality.

"Are you saying you're a different Oogami from the usual Oogami?"

"Bingo! Oh, except the full-moon me knows everything the normal Isaki sees and hears. The opposite is true, too. I can't keep anything a secret from her, either… So don't get any weird ideas, Mr. Hitoma."

"What kind of person do you take me for…?"

"Ha-ha-ha! I guess you don't have the balls!"

"Seems like you're quite capable of making a fuss all on your own. Oogami's going to get mad at you."

"Awww! But I like teasing you! I'll be back to the usual Isaki Oogami tomorrow, though. So you can relax. Don't get your panties in a knot."

She was smiling, but it sounded like she wished she'd disappear.

Isaki Oogami.

Werewolf. Enrolled six years ago and was promoted to the advanced class last year. Wants to become human to "graduate from this half-baked existence as a werewolf."

The bell rang, signaling the start of second period.

It was time for world history with the advanced class.

* * *

After class, Oogami skipped up to me.

"Hey, Mr. Hitoma! Which of these is cuter?"

In her hands were two lipsticks of the same color.

"...What's the difference?"

"*Excuse* me?! They're completely different! This one's coral pink. It's a gentle shade with a tint of red. And *this* one's blossom pink. It's soft like the color of cherry blossoms! Look! The coral is slightly richer in color! Can't you tell?!"

"Sure...?"

Both of them looked like the color of fish roe to me.

But if I told her the truth, I was sure to piss her off.

Displeased with my half-hearted attitude, Oogami puffed her cheeks up like a blowfish.

"Fine! Since today's a special day, I was gonna do you a favor and apply the shade you liked better! Y'know what, you seem like a nerd, so I picked these two, thinking you're into the innocent type, but maybe you prefer a bolder shade? Actually, forget that. What's your type? Oh, right, you're into jailbait, was it? That's what you said when you introduced yourself, right?"

"Wait, wait, wait, wait."

Way too fast. Slow it down already!

"First of all, I don't remember saying anything of the sort, and second of all, I am *not* into kids!"

"Really?!"

What do you mean, "Really?" These so-called shared memories of yours seem awfully spotty. Or is it just my introduction you're missing a chunk from?

"So? What's your type?"

"...Huh?"

I thought I'd managed to dodge the question I in no way wanted to answer, but she asked me a second time... Something about her smile felt intimidating.

"...Do I have to answer that?"

"Seriouslyyyyy? Yeah, you do! I wanna know all about you. I can only talk with you once a month, after all!"

Agh... She's guilt-tripping me...

I guess girls, Oogami included, like talking about romance...

Nothing for it.

"I like women who are...um...you know...soft and warm and bubbly..."

"Go on."

"Downturned eyes and long hair and lashes, looks good in a skirt, is on the shorter side..."

"Now we're talking."

"Pale skin; a gentle, cutesy, high-pitched voice; likes science; gives me cookies..."

"I see, I...see...? Huh? Aren't you being a little *too* specific?"

Her instincts were *sharp.*

Minazuki, who had been listening nearby, jumped in. "Could you possibly be talking about a specific friend or person you like...?!"

"Oh? For serious? Now you've got my attention."

Haneda sidled up to us, having scented something interesting.

Usami was the only one who looked bored. She had her head buried in her textbook.

"N-no! It's not like that!" I insisted.

"Methinks the lady doth protest too much! LMAO! I literally can't! No way! For real? Like, for real, real?"

"Isn't it easier just to 'fess up?" Haneda said.

"Indeed!" Minazuki added. "Love is a wonderful thing, in my humble opinion!"

They just wouldn't let up. A high school girl's appetite was like a piranha's when it came to gossip! Terrifying...!

"Anyway, now I know for sure Mr. Hitoma likes innocent girls. So, just for today, I'll doll myself up like a bad girl with a heart of gold."

A bad girl with a heart of gold? Does that kind of trope exist...?

"Oh, since I'm here and all, for once, let's eat lunch together! We'll meet here in the classroom. BYOL! Got it?"

I see that I don't have a choice.

Not that I had any reason to refuse, either. I told her, "Sure, sure," and left it at that.

Like this Isaki had said, it was a good chance for me to get to know this Oogami better.

There always seemed to be a distance between the usual Isaki Oogami and the other students. It had been bothering me for a while.

I was curious about her self-professed desire to escape her "half-baked existence," too.

Does that mean she wants to be rid of her dual personality? Will one of them have to disappear? Or would they merge? Do both of them agree to that?

Is this a goal that Oogami absolutely can't accomplish without becoming human?

* * *

When lunchtime rolled around, I decided to eat in the classroom as promised.

"Mr. Hitoma! Did you bring your lunch?" Oogami asked me when I entered.

"Uhhh, yeah."

It wasn't just the two of us. The whole class was there.

My main dish that day was bread. Actually, that was my appetizer and dessert, too. There'd been some sort of bread sale, and my mom had bought a truckload.

"What? You call this lunch?! It's all carbs! You have to eat some veggies! Okay, fine! I'll split some of mine with you! Here! Salad! Oh, I know—I'll feed you. That way you'll be more in the mood to eat, right? Open wide!"

"Wha—?! Guh!! Oogami—mmph…!"

"There we go. Eat up! Attaboy! Wa-ha-ha!"

What's so funny?! How can you laugh when I'm here choking *on the salad you force-fed me…? No, don't tell me!! Do you think I'm some kind of toy?! See? Minazuki keeps glancing at us like she doesn't know whether it's safe to look! Haneda's amused as always. And Usami's totally ignoring us…which is amazing in another sense!*

That was the rant I dearly wanted to deliver, but I couldn't say anything with my mouth full. I chewed through the salad with single-minded intent.

…What an odd texture. Oh, I know. This is the papaya salad. That's why it's so soft…

Come to think of it, she was talking about papaya earlier, right?

As I worked my mouthful, I carried on my meaningless back-and-forth in my head.

"Hmm? What? You're making a weird face. Oh, are you wondering about the papaya salad? That's what it is! I was curious 'cause it was trending on social media! The post said that papayas have an enzyme that breaks down sugars! So of course, I had to try it, right?! You should start watching what you eat, Mr. Hitoma, don't you think? You're not getting any younger."

She hit me where it hurt. Truth be told, I'd also been thinking about switching up my diet.

…But I just couldn't muster up the desire to eat salad. It was tasteless. Basically just a clump of mystery greens.

Nope, ramen is king! Ramen is life! I'll hit my vegetable quota by eating ramen! I'll show the world it can be done!

By the end of my internal monologue, I had miraculously managed to swallow the papaya salad.

"Oh, you're done?"

"Oogami...don't go shoving things into people's mouths... Eating that was rough..."

"Bwa-ha-ha! My b. ☆" She winked at me.

Is that what she calls an apology? Well, I'm not seriously angry, so I'll let it go.

Minazuki, who had been stealing glances at us the entire time, asked Oogami, "I'm fascinated by this papaya salad of yours! Won't you tell me the recipe next time?"

"No probs, Kyouka! Of course! It's surprisingly easy to make and so tasty! Oh! I'll send it to you now!" She took her phone out of her pocket and started tapping away rapidly.

"How delightful! I appreciate the speedy service!"

"Sent!"

"You're so fast, Isaki! I'd expect nothing less!"

Seeing the two of them so animated by their recipe exchange, I thought they looked like any other high school girls. I felt awkward, like I was the lone guy crashing a girls' brunch...

"...Hold on, you're allowed phones in school?" I asked.

"I mean, we've got some pretty strict filters, and the school checks all the data, but yeah, we still get internet," Haneda explained to me, sipping on a juice box.

"I see."

Their lifestyle seems surprisingly comfortable.

"I absolutely treasure the recipe you sent me last time, Isaki! The one for beauty!" Minazuki said.

"I remember! The chicken one?!"

"Yes! I often make it for dinner!"

"You're so good at cooking, Kyouka. Mad respect! You're an actual goddess!"

"I'm not that good! It's all thanks to you anyway! Please come and try my cooking again!"

"For sure! Thanks! Let's talk later!"

"With pleasure! I'll let you know!"

Were they cooking buddies? From their conversation, it seemed they both liked to cook.

I ate my bread as I listened. I brought a few different ones, but I found myself drawn to the baguette with the cod roe filling for some reason.

"Do you cook, Mr. Hitoma?" Oogami asked.

Drat. I wasn't expecting to have to field questions.

"Almost never," I answered.

"Ha-ha-ha! I knew it!! What do you do at home?"

"Play video games, I guess."

"You do seem like the type," Minazuki commented, and Oogami nodded vigorously.

What do you mean, I "seem like the type"? What type?

"How about you, Oogami? What do you do at home...or in your dorm, rather?"

"Me? I look up things related to beauty and watch videos about cute fashions and makeup! Oh! Right! I ended up picking the coral pink lipstick! It's adorbs, don't you think?" She pointed to her lips with a grin.

Ah, that's why I picked the cod roe baguette.

"Not bad. Looks tasty," I said.

"T-tasty?!"

...Huh?

What did I say just now?

A second passed.

"Wooow. I knew it! I just *knew* you were into jailbait!"

"No! Wait! You're wrong! It's not like that! It's a long story! I didn't mean *you*! I was talking about the roe! In the bread! It was a slip of the tongue, because... Aaagh, it's too much of a pain to explain!!"

"You're a real Humbert Humbert, Mr. Hitoma," Usami said.

"I didn't realize that was your type," Minazuki added.

"Yeah," said Haneda. "There's no defending yourself."

"Pile it on, why don't you?!" I protested.

They're usually all over the place. Why do they only band together in situations like this?!

After that, I desperately explained myself and somehow managed to clear up the suspicion that I was a pedophile. In exchange, I was branded as an ignoramus who was insensitive and oblivious about makeup.

Girls... Girls are so... Arghhh!

These girls might actually be better at surviving in human society than I am.

Actually, that's not quite right.

Not human society but female society.

Something I'll never have anything to do with all my life.

* * *

I'm defective.

The only one in the pack.

I'm the only one who's hidden away during the full moon.

Locked in a cold cell all alone.

Listen, Moon.

Is it my fault?

Did I do something wrong?

Why do the others in the pack call me a mongrel?

Why can't I be the same as everyone else?

Tell me. Why?

Why am I the only one who turns human when the full moon rises?

* * *

For some reason, it had felt like a particularly long day.

Actually, I suspected it was because I'd been dragged into Oogami's circle the entire time...

We had homeroom at the end of the day. Afterward, I let out a small sigh as I watched the students trickle from the classroom.

Oogami, being in the advanced class, was naturally an excellent student. Her full-moon counterpart, Isaki, was no different. However, if there was one thing that ate at me...

The person in question popped up in front of my eyes.

"Mr. Hitoma! What's with the sigh? Shall I gift you with some of my energy?!"

Perfect. I'd been meaning to talk to her.

"Do you have a minute, Oogami?"

"Whoa! Look at you, being so aggressive! Are we about to have a *moment*? A teacher and his student alone together in the classroom; who knows what'll happen? I'm game! I've got all the time in the world. So what are you going to do for me?"

"I want to talk about your reason for becoming human."

"Whoops, something just came up! Sowwy! ☆ Rain check! See ya next month!"

She stuck out her tongue and turned on her heel.

"Waitwaitwaitwait." I stopped her as she tried to dash out the door. "It's important."

"Ugh..."

Oogami glared at me resentfully, her ears drooping and her tail sweeping the floor. She was clearly displeased.

"...But, like, why bother? It's *my* reason. It has nothing to do with you."

"...!"

It has nothing to do with you.

Those words rendered me speechless.

Did I stick my nose into somewhere I shouldn't have again? Just like I did back then? Am I about to hurt another one of my students with my carelessness?

Memories of the past played through my head.

Oogami looked like she wanted to say something in response to my sudden silence. But in the end, she just mumbled resignedly, "God, whatever,

I get it...," and dropped back into her seat. "Well? What did you want to talk about?"

I hesitated for a moment, unsure if I was allowed to ask, before I broached the topic.

"...You said you want to become human to 'escape this half-baked existence,' but what exactly does that mean? Do you want to have only one personality?"

Oogami's ears twitched.

"Yeah, so?"

"Can you explain to me in detail?"

"Seriously? Do I have to?"

"...I'm not going to force you."

If she really didn't want to tell me, then that was that. I didn't have the kind of courage to push the issue further.

For a while, Oogami watched me with a torn expression. Then she let out a small sigh.

"*Sigh...* When you put it that way, I feel like I have no choice but to tell you... Look, if you think about it, anyone would hate the idea of their personality changing whenever there's a full moon. The other Isaki is no exception. Before enrolling here, I heard her say that she loathed me so much that she wanted to kill me. I was pretty bummed out back then. I mean, who wouldn't be? *Wow, she hates me* that *much*, I thought. But, like, *I'm* the one who isn't needed. I figured it's only right, I guess, that I give the other Isaki full control of this body. Plus, I love the other me. So I want to grant her wish."

"Her wish?"

She looked straight into my eyes and spat, "For me to disappear. For the usual Isaki to become the only Isaki."

I wondered how much of that was what the Oogami in front of me actually wanted.

She smiled sadly. "That's what the other Isaki wants."

There it is again. Once in a while, this Oogami makes this indescribable expression full of resignation...or maybe longing.

"…What about you?" I asked.

"Huh?"

"What do *you* want? I'm not talking about the usual Oogami. I'm talking about you, Isaki, who's here during the full moon."

"I…"

From what I had heard so far, it sounded like she was ready to sacrifice herself.

Does she think everything would be solved if she didn't exist anymore?

"It's…it's all my fault the usual Isaki has suffered this whole time. That's why I don't have the right to say anything."

"Suffered?"

Oogami peeked at me before she continued. "…Yeah. I'm a werewolf, but I'm different from the ones humans usually picture. Hmm, oh, see, those werewolves are human most of the time, and on the night of the full moon, they turn into wolves, right? I'm the opposite. Normally, I'm a wolf, and I live with the pack, but when the full moon comes, I become human."

She turned her sorrowful eyes on me. A wistful smile rose to her face.

"You see, Mr. Hitoma, the full-moon Isaki—me—has been human since I was born."

* * *

An old memory.

It's a memory of me dozing in my mother's embrace on the night of a crescent moon. She was warm and her tail soft.

"Hey, Mom? Why do I stop being me when there's a full moon?" I asked.

She froze for a split second. "…Our family has the blood of humans in us."

"Blood of humans?"

"Yes. Do you know what *ancestor* means?"

"Uh-huh! It's your mom's mom's mom!"

"That's right. Such a clever girl. You see, there was a human among our ancestors."

"A human!"

"That's why, every now and then...once in a true blue moon, a pup like you is born."

"Wow! Are there any other pups like me?"

My mother's words seemed to get stuck in her throat when she saw my innocent smile. Then she hugged me so tight, it hurt.

* * *

"Actually, my ears and tail disappear on the day of the full moon, but here at school, and only here, I get to be the same as the other Isaki."

Oogami tossed her head and shook her butt as if to say, *Just look at my cute ears and tail!*

"Do you want to be wholly human?" I asked.

"...Hmmmm, I don't know," she answered with a quirk of her lips, looking unsure. She then softly petted her tail.

She held it tenderly, like you would something precious.

"But, Mr. Hitoma, you see..." Her hand paused. She looked at me. "What I want is for the other Isaki to no longer have to suffer because of me. That's it."

I see. I think I'm starting to understand.

"You're attending this school so you can live as a human and as the not-full-moon Oogami. Is that right?"

"Pretty much."

"And that's what the Oogami I've been teaching all this time believes as well?"

"Huh? I think so... Mm, we share memories but not feelings or thoughts, so I don't know the details. If I'm wrong, just ask the other Isaki! Also, are we done here? I stayed here for you, but I'm actually very busy. I only have two hours of me time a month. There's makeup vids to watch, and I want to look up the latest trends, too. Oh, and do some shopping! Sorry, really!"

"Oh, yeah, sorry for holding you up."

Had I really asked everything I wanted to?
Soon, the moon will wane.

* * *

"Neener, neener! Human! You're a human, aren't you?!"

"No I'm not! I'm a wolf! I've always been a wolf!"

"I know the truth! My mom told me! She said you smell like a human! That's why it's weird for you to be part of the pack!"

"Freak!!"

"I'm not a freak! I'm a wolf! Look! I have ears and a tail and fangs! See?"

"They must be fake!"

"Let's give 'em a tug and find out!"

"No! Stop it!"

"Hey! What are you doing?!"

"Oh, crap! Run!"

"Let's go!"

"Mom…"

"Are you okay? What did they do to you?"

"Mom…! Why am I different from everyone else? Tell me—why do they all stay the same even when the full moon is out? Why is it just me? Why…?"

Why am I the only one who's different?

* * *

The next day, it rained for the first time in a long time.

I don't like the rain.

I internally cursed the sky for the downpour and the damp, swampy air as I took attendance that morning.

Oogami was absent. She wasn't feeling well apparently.

* * *

It was raining the day after, too. Maybe the rainy season had come early.

Oogami was absent again.

A little concerned, I asked the others how she had looked in the dorm. But no one had seen her.

She had replied when Minazuki knocked on her door, so she was in her room at least. That reassured me slightly.

Something doesn't seem right, though. I'll go check on her after school.

The dorms were set apart from the school building. I hadn't been there since my first day.

I was about to enter when I was stopped by a woman in an apron.

"Oh! Mr. Hitoma! Stop! Stop!"

It was the dorm mom, Roost Rep Ryouko.

"Teachers are forbidden from entering the dormitories! Didn't the principal tell you when you came here together on your first day?"

"Oh, I'm sorry..."

I vaguely remembered him saying something of the sort... There was so much to keep track of every day that I'd clean forgotten. Come to think of it, this was an all-female dorm. I had narrowly escaped being branded a pervert...

"Actually, I was a little worried about Oogami," I explained. "She's taken two days off in a row. When I asked the other students, it seemed like something might be wrong."

"Ah... You're here for Isaki..." Ryouko sighed deeply and turned her face down. "I'm concerned, too... I haven't seen her in two days... She's not eating the meals I'm making, either, so I've been tossing and turning over whether she's getting her nutrients... Some of the kids cook for themselves, but she's not the type, not outside of the full moon, at least. I checked in with her, but all she said was, 'I'm fine'... And I'm not in the position to meddle in their lives, you know? I've been racking my brain over what to do..."

I see. The conversation only gave me more reason to worry.

But given my own position, I couldn't enter the dorms.

On the other hand, it had been only two days. *Maybe Oogami will perk up and come back to school soon,* I thought.

I was still troubled, but I thanked the dorm mom for telling me about Oogami's condition and left the dorms.

Oogami didn't come to school once in the next two weeks.

* * *

The night of the new moon, 8:52 PM.

It was almost the summer solstice, but by evening, it was already pitch-black.

For once, I was still heads down at work, busy with preparations for class and paperwork. I was the only one left in the teachers' office.

Nice. I'm at a good stopping point. It's about time for me to head home… But before I do…

Teachers who stayed after hours were required to do a circuit through the building before they clocked out. That was the rule. They were responsible for telling any remaining students to go home and to inform any other teachers they were leaving.

Nearly all the lights in the building were turned off. I wasn't exactly raring to patrol a pitch-black school, but…rules were rules.

I took a flashlight and set out.

At night, it was chilly inside the school. The sound of my own footsteps echoed eerily.

Why'd I have to go and play that horror game yesterday…?

This perfectly normal darkness took on a frightening edge. I felt as if something was going to jump out of the shadows or a loud noise was going to blast me from nowhere—

My imagination started to get the best of me as I made my way through the halls.

There's no one and nothing here at this hour.

Calm down. It's all right…

If I clear this circuit, I'll finish the game…!

When I thought about it that way, the patrol started seeming kind of fun!

A real-life horror game! This kind of content would be sure to go viral! But wait, if I think about it, how is this any different from a test of courage—?

Claaaaaaaaaaang...

"Ack!!!"

A booming metallic sound echoed through the night. Had something fallen?

Instinctively, I stopped and pivoted in the direction the sound had come from.

I take it back.

This isn't fun at all. I wanna go home.

I resumed my patrol, jumping at even mundane sounds like a window rattled by a breeze.

The advanced class is right up these stairs.

Come to think of it, I opened the window to circulate fresh air through the room before I left this afternoon. Did I close it...? I don't remember.

No big deal. If I left it open, I can just close it now.

Maybe the sound earlier was from something coming in the window.

That'd be a pain to deal with.

I nervously slid open the door to the advanced classroom.

The window was firmly shut.

Phew. Good...

Right during that moment of relief...

Swoosh.

From the corner of my left eye, I saw a large shadow move.

I...didn't mean to see...

My blood ran cold in an instant, and my heartbeat grew louder.

A shadow. Of a person? Or—?

The horror game from the previous night flashed across my mind.

Wasn't there a bad ending where the player approaches a suspicious shadow only to get swallowed up?

Could this be the same shadow?

My heart pounded faster. I felt chilly, and my forehead broke out in a cold sweat. I tightened my grip on the flashlight.

I swallowed hard and sipped in a breath. I prayed that it was all my overactive imagination and resolutely turned to look at the shadow.

There was nothing there.

In the light of my flashlight was nothing more than the classroom wall.

Seriously…? Are my eyes playing tricks on me?

The tension I hadn't realized I was holding flooded out of me.

Is it the game's fault that I'm seeing things when there's nothing there?

I am a bit of a video-game addict. In any case, I'm glad there wasn't—

I turned around to find standing behind me a girl dressed in white with disheveled hair.

"Aaaaaaaaaggghhh!!!"

"Eeeyyyaaaaaaaaah!!!"

Oh god, oh god, oh god, oh god!!!!

I tumbled clumsily to the floor, taking a desk down with me.

I didn't mean to look…! This…this is a first…!

I never believed ghosts could possibly exist, but—I had accidentally seen it.

White clothing. Long, shaggy hair. She had shrieked in a high-pitched voice and flown away from me—

Huh? She flew away? Not toward me?

I slowly swung the flashlight in the direction the girl in white had run, to check what had happened.

*   *   *

There was a pair of legs.

"...M-Mr. Hitoma?"

The voice that called my name trembled, but mixed in with the distress was a hint of relief.

At the other end of my flashlight was a girl on the verge of tears in a large sweatshirt and shorts.

...*This nighttime invader doesn't exactly fit the horror tropes.*

That was my first glimpse of Isaki Oogami in two weeks. She looked like she had lost weight.

*   *   *

Beautiful. Blinding.

The day of the full moon.
Alone in the cell where it's supposed to be cold.
The human me looks up with my eyes at the moon floating in the night sky.

She's me but different.
She stares at the moon and sucks in a deep breath.

I wonder what she's thinking about.

The moon and I are the only ones who know about her. Even though she's so lovely.
No one else knows about her—just the moon and me.
But she is *so* lovely.

It's my fault.
If I become human, the wolf me will disappear.

* * *

Then there would be more people besides the moon and me who would see this beautiful human, wouldn't there?

* * *

I stood the desk I had knocked over back up. The two of us picked two chairs at random and sat down.

"Oh maaan...," I said. "I'm seriously sorry..."

Oogami straightened her glasses, her expression stiff. She apologized, seeming genuinely remorseful. "That's all right... It's my fault for being here at this hour..."

"Did you hurt yourself when you fell? Are you okay?"

"Thank you for your concern... I'm fine..."

...She's actively flinching away from me.

I had a mountain of questions about her absence and her reasons for being in the classroom so late at night, but I didn't know how to ask...

An awkward silence fell between the two of us.

Argh—I have to say something...

I desperately searched for the right words, but I came up empty.

"The window..." Oogami broke the silence first. "...It was open when I passed by."

Looks like I forgot to close it after all.

"Then I started wondering what the classroom was like at night..."

She'd given in to her curiosity. I could understand the feeling, the desire to explore. I myself was the type to comb through every nook and cranny of a game map.

If I had to pick one question to ask—

"This is the third floor...," I said.

How had she come in through the window...?

"Oh...I, uh..." Oogami opened and closed her mouth, but no words came out. She appeared reluctant to answer, but she finally admitted, "...It looked like I could make it, so I jumped. I climbed a tree and leaped off the branch."

She spoke so quietly, like she was confessing to a crime.

The crime in question was "on-campus unhuman-like behavior resulting from using one's bestial physical abilities."

In other words, it was cause for docking points.

I looked out the window as I considered how to deal with Oogami's misdemeanor. The curtains were open, revealing the night sky expanding beyond the glass.

Recently, we had been getting nothing but rain, so it had been a while since I had last seen the starry sky. Mr. Hoshino had told me that the Big Dipper and Spring Triangle were especially pretty this time of year, and without the moon, the stars seemed even more beautiful than usual.

"Oogami." I returned my gaze to my student. "Why did you come here at this time of night?"

According to my watch, it was 9:17 PM.

All the students attending this school lived on campus. If I remembered correctly, they were supposed to be back in the dorm by eight. Lights out was at ten, and at midnight, the rest of the lights in the building were turned off. Because of the scolding from the dorm mom I'd received last time, I had read through the documents relating to the dorms all over again, so I didn't think I was wrong.

Oogami gripped the sleeves of her hoodie, her face turned downward.

I patiently waited for her to speak.

The silence was uncomfortable, and I was tempted to say something, but at the same time, the silence had a different quality to it from the one between us before. I felt that if I were to speak, I'd rob Oogami of what she wanted to say.

The girl before me sat perfectly still. I watched her quietly.

I wonder how long we sat there for.

It felt like an eternity, but it was possible not even five minutes had passed.

Drip. A tear fell onto the back of Oogami's hand.

"Ah, s-so...sorry... I—I..." She wiped her eyes desperately, but she couldn't keep up. The tears spilled down her cheeks. "Th-this isn't... I'm sorry... I—I don't mean to trouble you... *Hic... Sniff...*" She choked out the words in between sniffles.

I found myself reaching to hug her, but I came to my senses just in time.

I was a teacher. I wasn't allowed to touch students unnecessarily.

...Remember your position.

I set my outstretched hand back down on my knee and balled it into a fist.

"It's okay. Don't worry." I tried my best to calm her down with soothing words. "You're not bothering me at all."

Then, in the school where we were alone, Oogami burst out crying, sobbing at the top of her lungs.

* * *

"Yes, that's correct. I want to get rid of my dual personality. That's why I want to become human. It's all right. Up until now, I've turned human during every full moon, so I'm confident I'll graduate quickly. I can't stay in my pack any longer... I realize that my mother and the pack elders can only protect me for so long. Food is scarce this winter, right? I'm sure everyone is hungry. It's a miracle I've survived all this time. So... that's why I'm going to become human. Ah-ha-ha! Is something wrong? You look so conflicted, Director... Huh? I can have two personalities and still become human? Thank you for your suggestion. Um, I...understand... but I also know that living beings—be they human or wolf—will attack those who are different from them. Isn't that right? If my personality changed only on the full moon...wouldn't that just make me a sitting duck? I don't want that to happen. I want to become human and live a life of blissful ignorance... That's why I want to have only one personality. It's wrong for two personalities to inhabit this body. So...I want to be one person. Please, Director. Make me human. I loathe who I am so much, I could kill myself."

* * *

"I didn't want to see anyone," Oogami said all of a sudden when her sobbing had died down to sniffles. "I'm bad when it comes to saying what's important. That's why she misunderstood."

I didn't agree with or deny anything Oogami said. I just listened quietly.

"During the last full moon, I heard you talk to the other me. She said I wanted to become human because I hate her so much that I wanted to kill her..."

She trailed off, her voice trembling, and looked down again. I waited for her to continue.

"...But there's no way that could be true... The one I hate is myself— the me you're talking to right now. I hate *me* so much, I just want me to disappear... I want to become human so *she* can be the one and only personality in this body."

Her eyes swam with tears.

"How...how could she possibly think she's the one I hate...? What does she think I've worked so hard for? All my efforts, all of it, were so I could give her everything. Why...why doesn't she understand? She's supposed to understand me the best! There's no way I would want to become human the way I am...! There's not a single good thing about me. I'm a coward. I'm weak. All I do is cause trouble for others and drag them down. I hurt the people I love. I run away from everything—even now, I can only whine and complain...! I've bothered you, too. I can't be kind to anyone! I'm selfish and never consider anyone else's feelings. I can't stand myself. I absolutely loathe myself...!"

"Oogami."

She twitched and then froze when I said her name.

Is she thinking that she said too much...? Is she worried I'm mad at her? Or maybe it's both?

"Humans misunderstand easily," I said.

"What...?" she said, her tone disappointed.

"We humans can only see what's in front of us, so we're forced to fill in the blanks with our imagination. That's how misunderstandings happen."

I'm the same. I pretend I know how others feel when, in reality, I just inter-pret their feelings however it suits me.

"That's why we have to use our words to communicate. We have to show others exactly what we want them to see."

If I had been able to do that back then, would I have been different?

"Before worrying about how opaque other people's feelings are, isn't it more important to make sure you can properly convey what you yourself are thinking?"

If only I'd been able to tell myself that back then.

"Oogami," I said, "won't you tell me and the other Oogami what you most want to say?"

It was important to me that she didn't make the same mistake I had.

It wasn't too late for her yet.

"I…I…" She trembled as she tried to figure out what to say. "I want to make the other me human."

"Go on."

"…She's more precious to me than anyone else… The way she devotes herself to the things she loves, I think that's amazing."

"Yeah."

"But…the thing I want to say the most… The one thing I want her to know… It's probably been the same all along, and that's the fact that…I…I…"

Oogami's eyes glazed over once more with tears.

"I love her…!"

A large tear spilled down her cheek.

"Good. Thanks for telling me."

I was sure they'd each been looking out for the other, which was why their signals had gotten crossed.

It's easy to overlook the things that are supposed to be the most obvi-ous. When push comes to shove, putting your thoughts into words is perhaps the most important thing to make sure you and another person understand each other.

Oogami continued crying.

But compared to before, her tears had transformed into something warm.

* * *

"...I'm really sorry."

"Hmm? I told you already. Don't worry about it."

The two of us were walking to the teachers' office.

Oogami's eyes were red and swollen from crying so much. We were going to fetch the ice packs kept in the office freezer, and I planned to raid the fridge while we were at it.

Aren't there still a few bottles of sports drinks left?

While she iced her eyes, Oogami mumbled, "...I've never gotten this upset before." Her voice was so soft, it was like she was speaking to herself.

"Huh."

"I'm sorry to put you through all this."

"Hey, you didn't do anything wrong. This is what it's like to be human."

I passed her a bottle of sports drink. I'd helped myself, but there shouldn't be any problems if I replaced it the following day. Oogami took it with a quiet "Thank you."

"Mr. Hitoma, I'll be back in school tomorrow."

"...It won't be too much for you?"

"No, it's okay. Earlier, when I went into the classroom, I realized I missed being there. *I want to come to school and keep practicing*, I thought."

"All right." I packed up my belongings and prepared to clock out. "Shall we get going? Ah, feel free to take that bottle with you."

"Oh, thank you."

It was late. The time was 10:05 PM.

Oogami stood up from her chair, holding her bottle, which was still two-thirds full, with both hands.

"I'll walk you back to the dorm."

"What?! No, that's all right! I…erm…" She averted her eyes, embarrassed. "I…can't go back through the front, because I…climbed out the window of the dorm, too…"

"…I see."

I wondered what floor her room was on. I didn't know, but I got the feeling that with her physical abilities, she would be able to get in and out no matter what floor it was.

"Okay. I have to follow the school rules when it comes to the 'on-campus unhuman-like behavior' violation and handle it accordingly, but the dorms are outside my jurisdiction, so I'm going to pretend I didn't hear anything you just said… Still, I'd feel like a criminal if I let a student wander around the grounds alone at this hour. At the very least, let me drop you off close to the dorm."

The dorm was on school grounds, so it was very unlikely anything would happen to her. So why had I insisted? Well, it was for my peace of mind.

Yep, that's all it is.

"Oh, by the way, the dorm mom was worried about you, too. Are you getting enough to eat?"

"More or less… The full-moon Isaki collected a bunch of diet recipes that I've been cooking and eating."

"'More or less' is better than nothing. I'm glad."

Oogami nodded. She looked relieved. I wrapped up my work for the day.

The last bus was at 10:40 PM. I should narrowly make it on time.

The two of us headed home.

* * *

The next day, the day after the new moon, the sun was shining.

I headed to the classroom to hold homeroom. By the time I arrived, Oogami was already there. Her expression was stiff, probably because this was her first time in a while coming to school. I was concerned, but I didn't want to pry so soon after our conversation yesterday. Besides, making a big fuss might actually cause her to feel backed into a corner.

Fortunately, the other girls acted the same as usual. Minazuki seemed a tad more…chipper? At this rate, it shouldn't be long before Oogami recovered her spirits.

I ran through the morning announcements and took roll call as I did every day.

The sun had peeked its face out for the first time in a long while, and its rays bathed the classroom gently in a warm glow.

* * *

June 11.

I suppose I should say, "Nice to meet you."

It actually is the first time I'm writing to you like this, so it's appropriate, I think.

Dear Full-Moon Isaki,

I overheard you when you spoke to Mr. Hitoma the day of the last full moon.

First, I would like to apologize for the misunderstanding.

I thought you would understand what I meant when I said I want to become human, because the one who is human is you. That's why I believed the word *human* was all that was needed to convey my desire to erase myself and leave everything behind to you.

But I was wrong.

You told Mr. Hitoma that you blame yourself for causing me pain.

And I always thought it was my fault that you were suffering.

Two birds of a feather, we are. There really was no way we could've understood anything without expressing how we felt with words.

The way I am now, I don't think there's any place I belong.

That's why I want to become human.

As for how we get there, I want to figure it out together with you.

Maybe it's not a bad idea for us to stay together, just like the director suggested back then. Recently, I've begun to think that.

I want to know more about your thoughts and feelings.
We're closer than any two people can be, and I think that's exactly why there's a lot about each other we don't know.

So will you share an exchange diary with me?
I look forward to a favorable response.

* * *

"I'm melting..."

It was a morning in late June.

The summer solstice had come and gone. That day, the rainy season was officially ending. It was earlier than usual, according to the weather report.

The sun was out in full force, bringing all the suckers in suits like me to the verge of death.

It's still morning, but the heat's already unbearable... I should break out my summer wardrobe. Won't the school adopt a business-casual dress code when it's hot out? Although, come to think of it, Mr. Hoshino doesn't wear a tie to begin with...

I was nearly at the office—in other words, the teachers' office.

The room was air-conditioned, so it was heaven. I had originally thought it would be rough on Ms. Saotome if we lowered the temperature too much, since she was a woman, but she said that if anything, she was more sensitive to heat.

"Ahhh... Can't wait to savor the cool breeze in the teachers' office— Gah!!"

"Hey, Mr. Hitoma. Lemme borrow you a sec, okay?"

"What?!"

By the time I had noticed the slippered footsteps pounding closer from behind me, the mystery assailant had already seized a fistful of my suit. Everything happened so fast, I ended up going along. Dragged by my suit, I found myself in an empty classroom on the third floor, into which I was shoved unceremoniously.

"Ack!" I yelped, stumbling over the step leading to the podium.

But my kidnapper paid me no mind and calmly shut the door.

"Why the sudden abduction, Oogami?" I demanded.

Showy makeup, disordered clothing, and a carefully styled mass of hair.

Right. It's the full moon today.

Oogami was fidgeting. Her expression was somewhere between angry and embarrassed.

"Look at this!" She shoved a notebook in my face. "Last month, I said some pretty awful things, didn't I? I thought the other Isaki hated me. And then the two of you ended up talking about all sorts of things, right? When I woke up this morning, I found this notebook on my desk. We share memories, so I didn't have to open it to know what was inside, but I still read it over."

She stroked the cover tenderly. It looked like your average college-ruled notebook the school distributed. Oogami the Rebel was the one I was talking to at the moment, but with the way she was gazing at the note-book, I thought she looked the same as the reserved Oogami.

She laughed softly. "We're starting an exchange diary, Mr. Hitoma! From now on, she and I are gonna tell each other all about what we're thinking and feeling! I want to stay together with the other Isaki! Oh, but I want to become human, too, so I can wear all kinds of cute clothing and try different cosmetics! That's why we're going to talk lots and lots in this diary and figure out what to do! Together!"

I had never seen her smile so brilliantly as she did then. I wondered if that was the effect of the sparkly makeup she was wearing.

She hugged the notebook carefully to her chest.

"Thanks for listening to me, Mr. Hitoma! I figured I owed you an update! That's all! Okey doke! I wanna research summer makeup looks, so I'm gonna head back to the classroom. Thanks! Keep watching me, okay? Stay tuned!"

After that whirlwind of an announcement, she bounced out of the room.

Where would the future lead her?

Deciding which road to take would surely require more than a day's work. I hoped the two Isakis would be able to talk things through and make a decision they were both satisfied with. I was positive they would be able to figure out the best path for them.

It was my special privilege as a teacher to be able to watch over them as they evolved.

It was about time for me to face my past, too.

The warm breeze brought in a fresh green scent through the open window. It was the smell of growing trees and verdant leaves.

Summer was nearly here.

A Misanthrope
Teaches a Class for
Demi-Humans

Mr. Hitoma, Won't You Teach Us About Humans...?

The Misanthrope and the Summer Vacation by the River

At last, the long-awaited summer!

Blue skies! White clouds! And my pasty self!

At the moment, I, a staunch believer of spending my holidays in the bastion of my own home, was out playing the part of student chaperone beneath the piercing rays of the summer sun.

How had I ended up in this situation…?

Our story begins before the start of summer vacation.

* * *

"Heeey, Mr. Hitoma, wanna go to the river over summer break. You know, the one at the edge of the forest," Haneda said to me one day.

"What river?"

"This one. Right here."

She pulled out a copy of the campus map. There was a river by the forest border, a slight distance from the main school building, right where she said it was.

I hadn't known. It seemed like a perfect hangout spot for the students.

"Nice. Go for it. Have fun," I said.

"You're missing my point. Be our chaperone," Haneda demanded.

"What?"

"This river is actually *just* outside campus."

"Really?"

If it was on the campus map, didn't that mean it was on the campus? I looked at the map again.

"You heard the principal earlier, right? 'Students may receive special permission to borrow the director's jeweled rings to leave the premises as long as your destination is within two kilometers of the border. You must apply two weeks in advance and be accompanied by a teacher.'"

"Someone was listening carefully."

"Heh-heh, I *am* an outstanding student, you know. Anyway, that's the gist. So any plans for the break, Mr. Hitoma?"

"Gaming at home."

"Got it. No plans. Good. I've already filled out the application. Sign here, please."

Haneda took out a second sheet of paper. *When did she put all this together...?*

The application was excessively detailed. Not only did it ask for the number of students going and their names, it asked for the ring sizes to be borrowed and the dates they would be needed in both the Gregorian and Julian calendars. It was practically a test. Only a student who could parse and answer the questions perfectly would be given permission. The application was likely part of the school's evaluation as to whether to grant permission.

"...Good job filling this out," I said.

Teacher instincts kicking in, I scanned the sheet. As far as I could tell, she hadn't made any mistakes.

"Hmm? It's nothing more than a form, though? Anyone can do it once they remember how," she replied.

As expected of an honor student.

I wanna try saying something cool like that.

"But this is for August eighth," I said.

"Oh, are you busy that day?"

"Uh, no..."

That was a lie. I actually did have plans.

August 8 was the day of our family reunion. Truth be told, I always felt out of place at those events. Getting together with my relatives was never any fun. Every year, I was swarmed by old men who had known me since I was a baby. They said all sorts of unnecessary things no one wanted to hear, like, "You've only ever had eyes for games, Rei-Rei," or, "Remember when you wet the bed that time you stayed over?" All I had were bad memories of these gatherings.

In that case, it might not be such a bad idea to join my students…but…

"I don't wanna go outside in the summer…," I demurred.

Haneda had no patience for my whining. "Seriously?" she said in exasperation. "You're a sad excuse for a teacher, Mr. Hitoma."

"Is Hitoma bailing on the application, Tobari?"

"Mr. Hitoma! It's cool and refreshing by the river!"

"Usami… Minazuki…," I said. "Refreshing, huh…? Hmm, well…"

I guess if all I need to do is be there, I could play my games under the shade of a tree… But I still have to get there… And the family reunion is a hassle… Gahhh…

"Just one more push," Usami said.

"Isaki! Full-Moon Isaki left me this note!" Minazuki announced.

Oogami jumped into the fray to persuade me. "R-really?! Shall I read it?"

What's this about a note from Full-Moon Isaki?

"*Ahem. 'Dear Mr. Hitoma,* ♥ *I picked out cute swimsuits for everyone. Tell me what you think!* ♥ *Get hyped for what you're going to see! You'd better come!* ♥'"

"No way! I can't possibly say yes to that!"

What an obvious trap!!!!!!!!! Don't dangle swimsuits in front of me!!!! That makes it harder to agree!!!

"You're overthinking, Mr. Hitoma!" Minazuki said.

"Don't you know the story 'The North Wind and the Sun'?" I asked.

That was right. At that moment, I was being battered by the north wind.

See, look. Usami's eyes are as cold as a blizzard.

I was just minding my own business, but I was being sliced to pieces.

Haneda surveyed the scene and lightly cleared her throat. "Jokes aside—"

Your jokes pack a punch...

"—we're tired of staying on campus and in the dorm all the time. Once in a while, it's nice to get away just for a bit! We want to see the outside world. Come on, Mr. Hitoma... What do you say?"

Guh... She's clearly trying to butter me up...

I looked at the advanced students. I passed in and out of the school every day, but I realized now that these girls couldn't leave campus unless there was a special occasion. That kind of life was good and all for a hermit like me, but...they were different.

"*Sigh...* Fine."

I relented.

They work hard. What's the harm in keeping them company now and then?

With the students watching over me, I penned my name in the field for "Chaperoning Teacher."

I handed the application back to Haneda, who took it with a grin.

"Perfect. Thanks, Mr. Hitoma."

She hummed in satisfaction as she ran a finger down the page, performing one final check. When she got to the bottom, she snapped her fingers.

"'Kay, everything looks good! Oh, right, Mr. Hitoma. We'll be meeting at nine at the front entrance. Don't you dare be late. I'm gonna go turn this in to the principal. Can't wait!"

Haneda dashed out of the classroom, freshly filled application in hand.

I wasn't thrilled to be going, per se, but at least I had gotten out of the dreaded family gathering. The outing was the perfect excuse, and I supposed I could call that a win.

That was how I ended up accompanying my students one day during summer vacation.

* * *

"What took you so long, Mr. Hitoma?" Haneda drawled.

"He was definitely up late playing games," Usami said.

August 8, nine o'clock AM. I squeaked into our meeting spot at the last second.

"No, you're all just early," I argued. "It's summer vacation. Isn't it normal to stay up late and sleep in?"

"Is it?" Minazuki asked.

"Only for Hitoma," Usami replied.

"I *said* you'd better not be late," Haneda chided.

"Uck…I'm the minority here…"

Oogami came to my defense. "Oh, I—I understand! You end up lazing around at night, since there's no reason to wake up early!"

"Oogami…! That's exactly right…!"

"Okay, whatever, Mr. Hitoma. Can you go and get the director's rings from the principal already? We can't leave the barrier without them. You know what happens if we try, right?"

"Oh yeah. You go back to your regular appearances? Instead of what you look like now. Is that right?"

"Ummm, more or less. If we leave without the ring, we'll return to the way we were before coming to this school, and we won't be able to reenter the barrier without it. That's why the rings are super-*duper* important. As chaperone, your job is to watch over us, but an equally big part of your responsibility is to take care of the rings. Remember that."

Having judged me unreliable, Haneda took careful aim at me and slapped me with a strict warning.

Looking back, I remembered the principal had told me about the rings on my first day, too… The ring had been sitting on my left pinkie ever since.

A silver ring with a red jewel embedded on the inside.

I told Haneda I'd be careful and then headed to the principal's office.

* * *

"Mr. Hitoma! I was waiting for you," the principal said. He was round as always.

As I took in his appearance, he bustled to the safe in the corner of the office.

"According to the application, you'll be needing four rings, is it?" he asked.

"Ah, yes. That's right."

Haneda, Usami, Oogami, and Minazuki made four. There was no mistake. The principal took out four beautifully decorated, small boxes and gave them to me.

"In the unlikely event that you lose these rings, the blame is going to fall on your shoulders, so be very careful," he warned. "If you lose them... you'll be severely—and I mean *severely*—punished."

"Punished...?"

Damn. These rings are growing heavier and heavier.

Somehow, I'm starting to dread going.

"The director would decide what exactly would happen to you based on the circumstances, so I can't say exactly what the punishment would be. Anyway, take good care of them...!"

"Y-yes, sir!"

Again with the director...

The first semester was already over, but I had yet to meet the director. I wondered who they were.

Are they even human? Nothing would surprise me from this school... Who or what could they be?

As I mused upon the director's identity, I returned, holding the four boxes, to the entrance where the advanced students were waiting.

"That was quick," Haneda said, rising to her feet from her seat on the stairs and walking toward me. "Ooooh, those the ring boxes? Thanks."

"Yeah, here."

Each box had a sticky note with a student's name written on it. I distributed them accordingly.

The girls eyed the boxes curiously.

"These will allow us to leave the barrier in our current forms...!" exclaimed Minazuki.

"...I'm getting nervous," Oogami said.

"We'll be matching with Mr. Hitoma. Makes you think," Haneda said.

"Can we put them on?" Minazuki asked me.

"Go ahead."

That's right. Their ring sizes were written on the application form…

The rings fit them perfectly.

I hadn't told the school my size, and mine hadn't come in a box but an envelope. There had been comparatively little fanfare, so I'd nearly forgotten about the whole episode. However, seeing how happy they were, it hit me once again how precious the rings actually were.

"Great," I said. "Let's head out."

To the river just outside the barrier we go.

Off to make summer memories with the advanced class.

* * *

"Geez! You got me, Tobari!" Minazuki shrieked.

"Ah-ha-ha! The water loves you, Kyouka!"

"Usami!" Minazuki shouted. "I know you're there!"

"Heh, how naive. I'm over here!"

Half dozing atop a vinyl sheet with my head pillowed on my bag, I watched the students play around in the water.

On the way to the river, we had been misled by the signposts and had ended up taking a long detour, so I was knackered. I hoped someone would fix the signs by next time, though who knew if there was going to be a next time.

"Mr. Hitoma? You've been napping this whole time. Are you tired?"

A busty babe in a swimsuit popped up right in front of me.

I jerked in surprise. "Agh! I-I'm fine."

"M-Mr. Hitoma…? You seem pretty energetic, actually…?" Minazuki said, perplexed by my sudden burst of energy.

Y-you've got it wrong… I just don't have any defenses against swimsuits…

"I—I guess… Forget about me. It's more important that you all are having a good time…"

"Hee-hee! Thanks to you, we are! I know all about the ocean, but I have a rather shallow understanding of rivers. They're wonderful, too!

Playing in the water is all the more enjoyable, since the swimsuits Isaki chose for us are so lovely!" Minazuki twirled around in a circle.

"Really…? I don't know anything about women's swimsuits…"

She pouted. "Yes, they're amazing! How can you not see?!"

Her stark shift in demeanor tugged at my heartstrings just a bit.

That's not it, Minazuki. I'm not lying when I say I'm ignorant about swimsuits, but the real reason I can't compliment you sincerely is because it could count as sexual harassment. I'm obligated to keep mum…!

Minazuki sulked, despondent, but in the next moment, her expression lit up again like she had been struck with a brilliant idea.

"I know! For your benefit, I'll present everyone's swimsuits to you! Full-Moon Isaki went to all the trouble of picking them out for us!"

"Wha—?!"

Um…?! Is this aboveboard?!

As I agonized, Minazuki barreled on.

"Isaki said she wanted to hear your opinion, too! Plus, she searched through everything from classic styles to the latest fashions to find ones that would look best on each of us! It's marvelous how much she loves fashion!"

Yeah, I can picture that. It seems like the kind of thing Oogami the Rebel would like.

"Great! Starting with mine, this is a classic halter-neck bikini featuring a popular multiple-straps design. The interlaced straps and the crisscrossing style are very trendy. The tantalizing peek of skin is sure to steal your breath away! …Is what Isaki said!"

I didn't really get it, but I could see that there were indeed a lot of straps. And like she said, the swimsuit teased what was underneath. It was a design you saw often on pinup models and spicy illustrations of bombshells.

Long story short—it was a spectacular design.

"Next! Usami is wearing a white one-piece with ruffles! The white frills go perfectly with Usami's fair complexion, and the translucent sleeves and ribbon on the back are just darling!"

At a glance, Usami's swimsuit looked like the kind of high-coverage design that a child would wear.

However, the back was actually very low-cut. The innocent, cutesy design of the front contrasted with the back's bold, mature design. Anyone who dropped their guard would find their heart skipping a beat when Usami turned around.

"Tobari is wearing a high-neck bikini! A mature design that bares the neck and collar. This style is also in right now, apparently!"

The design was exactly as Minazuki described. The swimsuit was simple and dynamic. Because of the high neck, its visual center was higher than other swimsuits, which had the effect of accentuating Haneda's bare stomach.

Well…the design draws the eyes in. It can't be helped if I stare.

"Isaki's swimsuit is an off-the-shoulder bikini, a style that is slowly becoming a classic. It's decorated with ruffles. Full-Moon Isaki agonized over what to pick before landing on this one. She figured the usual Isaki wouldn't overly mind this particular design! It features an understated but feminine black gingham pattern, striking the perfect balance between cute and mature! How amazing!"

Right on the money again. It was a bold but cute swimsuit.

…Off-the-shoulder tops don't cover the shoulder and collarbones, right? Maybe it's just me, but won't they slip off?! Isn't it super risky?!

…That's what I thought every time I saw one. There's the reasoning that as long as you have large boobs, your chest will keep it from falling down! Was that it…?

"Um, Kyouka." Oogami waded our way right as we were talking about her. "Since you're telling Mr. Hitoma about swimsuits, I wanted to come and say my thanks… Um, during the last full moon, you talked a lot with the other me while she picked everything out. Thank you so much!"

"Oh, please! I had fun, too! More important, the swimsuit looks great on you, Isaki! It's so cute! Gorgeous!"

Oogami squatted down and curled into a ball, flustered at being complimented to her face. "Erm, really…? You mean it?"

Minazuki squatted, too, and looked Oogami in the eyes. "I do! I have never lied in my entire life," she said seriously.

They locked eyes and simultaneously broke out laughing.

"Ha-ha, that's a lie," Oogami said.

"Oops, you caught me."

The playful atmosphere became hard for me to stand. I didn't know what to do with myself.

…There's nothing for me to do here, and I don't know where to look. Let me go find a tree farther away to sit under.

I started packing up the sheet and bags to leave when Usami asked, "Where are you going, Hitoma?" She was holding on to a large floatie.

"Oh, it's getting hot over here, so I was thinking of moving into the shade," I explained.

"Hmm… Okay, I'll help."

"Huh?"

That was unexpected. What kind of turn of events was this?

I stared at Usami and failed to hide my surprise.

"…What?" she said flatly.

"Ah, nothing…"

"If you've got something to say, then spit it out." She was disgruntled as always, but she was swiftly and neatly gathering the belongings I had scattered around the sheet. "I bet you're thinking it's unusual for me to help you."

Oof, bull's-eye…

"…We made you accompany us on your day off, so I figured I would give you a hand."

Usami…you have a soft side after all…

"It could end up being a chance to raise my grade," she added.

Nope. Business as usual. But nevertheless…

"…Thanks for the help, Usami," I said.

She picked up the smaller of the bags, stone-faced as usual.

I shouldered the sheet and the heavier bag filled with who-knows-what and carried them over to the shade underneath the trees.

That'll do it.

"Operation Relocation complete!" I announced.

"What a lame name."

"You don't get it, Usami. Short, sweet, and to the point is key here."

"Really...?" She looked at my new base, half baffled.

I called it a base, but it was just the same vinyl sheet with the bags placed on top.

"Mr. Hitoma?" Haneda came over to join us at the reconstructed base. "You moved. It's nice here under the shade."

"Usami helped," I said.

"Wow, look at you go."

"You were a big help, really. Thanks," I told Usami. "Now I can play my game to my heart's content!" I sprawled out across my newly built base and took my handheld console from my bag.

"...Someone's enjoying himself," Usami said.

"...Seriously," Haneda agreed.

I was looking at my screen, but I didn't have to see them to know that they were rolling their eyes at me.

"We've come all the way here. I'm going back to the river," Usami declared.

In my periphery, I saw her pick up her floatie and drink.

"You do you. Have fun. Be careful," I called to her.

"You're the one who should be making sure we're careful!"

"She's right, Mr. Hitoma," Haneda said. "Actually, you should come and play with us. You're already here."

"No can do. I didn't bring a swimsuit."

"What a prude."

It has nothing to do with being a prude. I don't have what I don't have.

"Are you taking a break, Haneda?" I asked.

"Hmm, yeah, sure."

"Okay. Running around that much will tire anyone out."

Although, when I checked from the corner of my eye, Minazuki and Oogami were still fooling around. In the shallows, Usami was lying on her floatie, staring vacantly up at the sky.

"Um, hey," Haneda said with a somewhat bashful expression. "Thanks for today."

What's with the sudden sincerity?

While I was puzzling over how to respond, Haneda went on. "I wanted to make some memories while we can. Once this summer is over, it's over. One of us could graduate and leave." A corner of her lip ticked upward. "We don't know what'll happen yet, though. And besides, Minazuki likes to splash around in the water, so I wanted to bring her here."

"I see."

To be honest, I hadn't wanted to go anywhere in the heat, but now I realized that the scenery was beautiful and the riverside cool. Plus, for some reason or another, I got to catch up on the latest trends in women's swimsuits—although I guess I could've done without that last one.

Anyway.

"I'm glad you're enjoying yourselves," I said.

And I'm glad I could escape my dreaded family reunion.

"Mr. Hitoma! Watch out!"

"Ack!!!" A blast of water splashed over me, soaking my upper body.

Thank god I opted for the waterproof console...

"Oh no, oh no, oh no! I'm so sorry, Mr. Hitoma...! Are you all right?" Oogami beseeched me with tears in her eyes. She'd sprayed me with her water gun, most likely by accident.

"Ah, I'm fine, Oog— Gwahhh!!!"

Beside me, Haneda had turned on me and shot me with her own water gun. "Ah-ha-ha! You should see your face, Mr. Hitoma!"

"What's so fun about getting me soaking wet...?"

"What do you mean? It's hella amusing." Haneda grinned mischievously, hoisting the squirter.

This kid... She's the kind who gets a kick out of messing with people.

"I want to play Smash the Watermelon," Usami piped up. At some point, she had left off her slow cruise on her floatie and had come back to shore.

"Splendid idea! I'll bring over the watermelon!" Minazuki volunteered, hurrying to her own bags.

"Don't trip!" I warned her.

"Thanks for your concern!" She took a small watermelon out of her backpack.

Aaaah, summer.

Summer, to me, meant unbearable heat, a season best forded playing games at home.

But, you know, once in a while...

Just for a single day, it wasn't so bad to spend a holiday out in the sun.

A Misanthrope
Teaches a Class for
Demi-Humans

Mr. Hitoma, Won't You Teach Us About Humans...?

The Misanthrope and the Angel's Comet

A MISANTHROPE TEACHES A CLASS FOR DEMI-HUMANS

"Usami! Listen, listen! My teacher complimented me today! She told me, 'Seiko, your letters are the prettiest'!"

Wow, that's great.

"And guess what? I can write the whole alphabet now! I'm sooo happy. Let me give you a pet. Heh-heh, you're so soft, Usami. Cutie-patootie."

I know. It's because you take good care of me.

"Come on! You should sleep with me today, too!"

Fine. What would you do without me, Seiko?

"Love youuu, Usami! Let's stay together always!"

Duh. Obviously.

I love you, too, Seiko!

* * *

Six months had passed since I started working at this school.

September 1. The beginning of the second semester.

The first day back after summer vacation, the students weren't the only ones in a funk. The teachers were the same. I, too, would rather spend my entire life gaming if possible…

Studios tended to release new games and bonus content during the summer, so for better or worse, I'd lived it up over the holiday.

Man… If only there was such a thing as unlimited time! I know it's all a marketing ploy, but I'll still buy the games! Take my money!! Take all of it!!!

I'd hoarded games and burned through them. Those were the days. *Heh-heh... That was the best...*

"Ewww. What are you smirking about? Gross."

"Wh-who's smirking...?!"

Damn. I completely dropped my guard.

I had been on my way back to the classroom after the opening ceremony for second semester, daydreaming about my fun summer memories, when I found myself caught in the disgusted glare of a rabbit, aka Usami. Her icy gaze made me flinch.

"Anyone can tell you're fantasizing about summer vacation," she said. "I bet you spent it like a slob."

"...Do you think teachers get the same vacation as the students?"

"They don't?" she asked with a guileless expression.

Oho, just because you guys dragged me out to supervise you for a day, you think teachers don't have anything to do over the summer break? Admittedly, it's rare for me to get out, and it was kind of enjoyable... Plus it was my first time eating watermelon in a while. It was delicious— Wait a second! I'm getting distracted!

I cleared my throat exaggeratedly. "Yeah. When you're all on vacation, we teachers have to come to work as usual. Between paperwork and training courses, we still have plenty on our plate in the summer." I shook my head disparagingly. "You have much to learn, young grasshopper," I added, acting the part of a light novel protagonist.

A trace of guilt broke through Usami's usual poker face. She seemed to think she had said something offensive.

Whoops, might have overdone it.

"So then you were working during summer vacation?" she asked.

"Not all the time. I took a ton of days off," I confessed, caving after seeing Usami's expression.

You heard it here first, folks. It was ridiculously easy to take time off at this school...!!

* * *

Over the summer holidays, I took a whole—wait for it—three weeks off! Three weeks of bingeing games nonstop at home in a cool room…!! Day after blessed day of playing through the indie games I had hoarded over the mad rush that was the first semester, sometimes at the expense of sleep and food…!! It had been the pinnacle of depravity and the ultimate vacation!!

"…Flexing how busy you were when you were actually playing around is seriously lame. You disgust me," she said coldly before briskly walking into the classroom.

Ugh… I definitely overdid it…

When I saw Usami slumped at her desk, in a dreary mood, I felt a twinge of regret.

"…I wasted my time worrying."

Her voice was so soft, meant for no one's ears but her own.

* * *

Back in the classroom after the opening ceremony for the second semester, I noticed there was one person missing.

"Hmm? Where's Haneda?"

Tobari Haneda was the only one not in her seat. She'd looked drowsy during the ceremony, but she had definitely attended. I wondered what had happened.

Did she take a detour? Or could it be that she ran into trouble…?

While I was fretting over her absence, the door rattled open.

"Oh, sorry! Sorry I'm late. I found something rare," Haneda said.

"Haneda…what's that in your hand…?" I asked. "Wha—?! Uck! Gross!!"

She was holding something that was too stomach-turning to even describe.

It was a bug.

From its joints sprouted a mushroom. No, it was…being eaten away by the mushroom…?

It was disgusting. Absolutely repulsive.

I guess Haneda's the type who doesn't mind touching bugs...? Ohhh, because she's a bird... No, hold on. I don't want to talk about or see anything more than this.

For those curious, you can google it for yourself, but anything you see is on you.

"It's a caterpillar fungus," Usami said.

Unlike me, who had broken out in goose bumps from the top of my head to the tips of my toes, the other girls crowded around Haneda.

Caterpillar fungus? Sounds familiar. I feel like maybe it was a rare item in some game.

"This is my first time seeing one in person!" Oogami said. "So this is what they look like in real life."

"Me too!" Minazuki exclaimed. "I'd heard of them before, but apparently, they actually do exist! Fancy that!"

Erm... Why are you guys so excited by a bug shroom...?

The advanced students hovered over the abomination, clamoring excitedly as if they were talking about makeup...

Haneda stood in the middle of the throng, looking smug. "Heh-heh, I picked it up in the woods near school. Hey—how about you all play a game with me with *this* as the prize?" She smirked mischievously.

"Let's do it!" Usami said.

"I'll play!" said Oogami.

"I would love to join, too," Minazuki added.

It seemed that everyone was going to participate. Gamemaster Haneda decided the rules on the spot. I was happy to see all of them so excited.

But they had forgotten one thing.

"You guys—" My voice seemed to trigger their memories, and a guilty expression stole over each of their faces. "I'd love to start class sometime soon, if you please."

And so, together with the bug shroom, we began the second semester.

* * *

After school, Usami ended up winning Haneda's game.

"Yes! The caterpillar fungus is mine!" she cried.

I've never heard her this happy before...

It was a stark contrast to her usual attitude. The elated Usami was a refreshing sight to see.

"Congrats! Here you are. One caterpillar fungus," Haneda said.

Usami took her prize. "Thanks!"

I still had no idea what all the fuss was about.

That...that thing *is seriously gross...*

"Hey, Oogami," I said.

"Yes, what is it...?"

"What's so great about that bug shroom?"

"You call yourself a teacher when you don't even know the effects of caterpillar fungi? Idiot," Usami spat disdainfully, having overheard me. She was cradling the monstrosity carefully in her hands.

"It's not my expertise, so no. Actually, why in the world do you know about it?"

"In the human world, caterpillar fungi is used as a remedy in traditional Chinese medicine," Oogami explained to me politely, unlike Usami's response. "It's usually prepared alongside meat. Um, if I remember correctly, it's beneficial for the lungs and...kidneys? Something like that! It's an effective medicine." She smiled warmly, but I heard her mutter under her breath, "I wanted it, too."

Despite its appearance, it was actually a precious medicinal commodity. In that case, it made sense why they all wanted it...maybe?

Nevertheless, in this situation, you could definitely see a hint of the difference between these girls and "normal" high school students.

But, well, even among us humans, there were people with bizarre hobbies, and...being knowledgeable about a bug shroom didn't seem so unusual.

I wonder if my shampoo-taste-critic friend is doing well.

If I thought about it, the hobbies of some humans were definitely more extreme.

* * *

"Ahhh, that was fun," said Haneda. "Let's play again if we find another one."

"I wanted the caterpillar fungus for my above-the-sea collection," Minazuki said.

"It'd be a waste as a display piece. You have to put things like this to their proper use," Usami protested.

"My, are you feeling unwell, Usami?" Minazuki asked.

Usami's eyes seemed to soften at the question. "Not me." Her voice was gentle. Her usual moody expression cleared slightly.

She held the caterpillar fungus delicately, as if it were a fragile piece of treasure.

"It's for someone who's precious to me."

* * *

It was a little while after the second semester started, right after I had recovered from my summer-vacation blues and had begun falling back into my normal routine.

After school, the principal came up to Usami and me. Outside, it was still as bright as if it was noon.

"Usami, Mr. Hitoma, please follow me to my office. I have important news."

Like usual, his tone sounded somewhat joking, but he was wearing an odd expression.

He wants Usami, too?

Is he going to give her a warning about her behavior? No, that can't be it.

From my perspective as her homeroom teacher, I felt that the only thing Usami could stand to improve was her choice of words. As far as class went, she was always serious about her studies. It wouldn't be an exaggeration to say she made no mistakes. As for her language, to my knowledge, it wasn't a major problem. I gave her light warnings whenever she went too far.

Then, what could the principal want? Usami lacked her usual energy and followed the principal to his office quietly.

"…What? Stop staring at me," she snapped.

Oh, good. There's the fire I expect from her.

"Go on in," the principal urged us.

The wax figure who I had met during my interview was standing in a corner of the room as always. The expensive-looking decorations glittered.

Every time I came here, I was struck anew by the tastelessness of the room.

Huh? Did he get more wax figures? Was the one by the door there the last time I was here…?

Strangely, my steps seemed to drag. In contrast, Usami flitted quickly to the chairs in the reception space in the middle of the room and plopped into one. I sat down next to her.

The principal eased himself into the seat facing us. He took his time to speak.

"I have news about Seiko Kizaki."

Seiko who?

Usami leaped up and slammed her hands down on the desk. "Did something happen to Seiko?" she demanded, shoving herself forward. She looked about ready to grab the principal.

Usami was so close to him, he must've been able to feel her breath on his face. But he was unperturbed by the distance and continued calmly. "…The director received word about her. She's not young anymore, and her health has been declining. Recently, when she went in for a checkup, she was diagnosed with a serious illness. She's been admitted to the hospital."

"…How is she doing?" Usami asked.

"It's not looking good."

Usami went rigid. Her eyebrows furrowed, and her lips flattened into a line.

"…Seiko…," she mumbled, her voice trailing off. Her face was downturned. She balled her hands on the desk into fists.

"Therefore, after consulting with the director, we've decided to grant you a special privilege."

Usami's head snapped up. Anticipation and anxiety mingled on her face. "Special privilege…?"

"Two hours' leave."

"I can go and meet Seiko?!" she blurted out excitedly.

But the principal's expression was still dark. "Yes, however"—his glasses glinted eerily—"not in your current state. You will have to meet with her as you looked prior to enrolling at this school."

The principal's voice reverberated through the garish office. Usami swallowed heavily.

After urging Usami to make her decision quickly, the principal excused her.

Then it was just him and me in the office.

"Um, is Seiko Kisaki—?" I began to ask.

"She's the reason Usami wants to be human."

I knew it.

"I was torn over how much to tell you. There is the matter of confidentiality, you see. Apologies for the late explanation. Seiko Kizaki, seventy-eight years old—she's Usami's owner."

Owner? Oh, as in "pet owner."

"If Usami submits a formal agreement to exercise the privilege, I'll take her to Ms. Kizaki. I wanted you to attend this meeting because you're her homeroom teacher, and I wanted you to be aware of the circumstances."

* * *

I exited the principal's office and returned to the classroom to pick up some papers I'd left there. In the meantime, I mulled over what I had learned about Usami.

Sui Usami. Rabbit. She had been at the school for three years. Like Minazuki, she'd advanced to the next level every year. Wants to become human to repay a debt.

The human she wanted to repay was most likely Ms. Kizaki.

In the worst-case scenario, if by some chance Ms. Kizaki's condition suddenly took a turn for the worse and Usami became unable to pay back her debt, what was she going to do? How exactly did she plan to repay Ms. Kizaki to begin with? The vague goal was at odds with Usami's personality.

Usami was prickly and harsh toward others, but she was even harsher with herself.

She worked harder than anyone else.

Her academic performance and general conduct were unimpeachable. As long as she avoided getting too many points deducted for her sharp tongue, she could very well graduate this year.

That was the current state of things.

Usami would probably take the offer.

As far as I knew, the privilege that had been granted to her was the best that this school, which existed outside reality, could offer under the circumstances.

As she was, with her bunny-girl appearance, Usami was sure to attract attention both good and bad. That was why the principal had added the requirement that she had to go in her previous form, I imagined.

I arrived at the advanced classroom.

That was right. The students didn't originally appear the way I was used to seeing them.

I opened the door.

"You're still here?"

Inside the room, I found Usami all alone staring out the window, lost in her thoughts. From outside came the laughter and chatter of other students. When she noticed me, she turned my way.

"Hitoma… Mr. Hitoma," she said. It was the first time she had used a proper form of address with me.

"Usami, hey," I said. "I'm sorry. I barely know anything about your situation, so I'm not sure what to say. But the principal said you can exercise the privilege at any time, so—"

"There's no point." Usami's pretty features contorted. "If I have to meet Seiko in my original form, there's no point." Between the tremble in her voice and her teetering posture, she looked like she was going to fall apart at any second.

"...Of course there's a point, Usami. You're a rabbit, right? You can meet with her, cuddle up to her, and purr to let her know how you feel, can't you?"

She might not be able to talk with Ms. Kizaki the way we were doing now, but there was plenty she could do. Her presence alone would speak volumes, wouldn't it?

But Usami seemed only more pained. She glared at me.

"...You don't know anything, Hitoma... I...I...!" Her red eyes blurred with tears. "I can't snuggle with her or purr or share my warmth with her, not like a *real* rabbit would...!"

She cast her gaze over the desks in the classroom, one for each of the four advanced students.

"...I'm so jealous of everyone. Minazuki might not be able to stand in front of us in her original form, but she can reach us with her voice. Tobari can fly to wherever she wants. Isaki was basically human to begin with. It's not fair!"

I couldn't see Usami's eyes, hidden as they were behind a curtain of her hair—but the corners of her lips were curled upward in a sad smile.

"I...I'm not a living thing."

And living things can't move on their own. Which meant...

"I'm not a real rabbit. I'm a stuffed animal."

* * *

"Usami! Guess what! There's a boy I have a crush on!"

Oh yeah? What's he like?

"His name's Kenichi—I call him Ken—and he sits next to me! I had to run an errand for my teacher and bring all of the class's notebooks to the teachers' office, and he helped me carry them! Plus, he said the book I like was cool, and, and...when he smiles, I feel so happy!"

...This lovey-dovey talk is embarrassing.

"Also, the other day, we went and got a Calpico together... Hee-hee! I was so nervous, I couldn't taste a thing. Oh, but when he saw what I was wearing, he said it was something his little sister would wear! Was he calling me childish? How rude!"

What an inconsiderate jerk. But you seem happy.

The only thing I can do is listen to your stories.

That's why...as annoying as he is, I hope he'll make you happy.

* * *

After Usami confessed she was a stuffed animal, she quietly took a deep breath. It looked like she had decided something.

"Hitoma."

The uncertainty in her eyes from earlier when she had been alone in the classroom was gone. She stared straight at me, her gaze piercing.

"I want to meet Seiko as I am now," Usami declared. "But the principal and the director won't allow it."

...I have a bad feeling about this.

"So I want your help, Hitoma."

"...What exactly do you mean?"

"I want to borrow the director's jeweled ring that you're wearing."

"Usami...do you understand what you're proposing?"

With the ring, she'd be able to leave the barrier in her current form. However, she would be breaking the rules. And the consequence for that was:

"It's going to be harder for you to graduate."

Advancement and graduation in this school were determined based on a point system. Anyone found guilty of a rule infraction would have their points deducted.

"...Aren't you at this school because you want to graduate?"

"I want to become human in order to stay by Seiko's side!" Usami said firmly. She interlaced her fingers tightly in front of her chest as if she was praying. "Hitoma...I'm running out of time! I might lose Seiko! You're the only one I can count on! I'll do anything if you'll help me...! So..."

Her voice was choked with tears by the end.

Faced with this desperate Usami, I was at a loss for what to do.

"Hitoma, won't you help me out...?"

Her teary plea brought back memories of a different time.

Of a different student who had asked me for help.

The student who had betrayed me—the one I hadn't been able to save.

Usami peered anxiously at me after I fell silent.

"Hitoma...?"

My breathing grew shallow, and cold sweat pooled across my forehead and back.

I...

"I got it," she said. "Come with me. It'll be no different from being a chaperone. I won't go off alone. I'll stay where you can see me. It'll be fine—it won't be scary with the two of us together."

Why is Usami saying that?

Does it look like I'm going to refuse because I'm afraid of something?

Afraid?

Yeah, I am afraid. I'm afraid I'm going to cause another student anguish. I'm afraid of becoming the cause of someone else's misfortune. I'm afraid of being betrayed. If that's what's going to happen, it's much better for me to stay by myself without getting involved with anyone. When I try to help someone, I only end up causing trouble for others.

I can hear someone crying far away. The biting cold, a winter's classroom. A student yelling at me in tears.

I'm sorry. I'm to blame. It's all my fault. It's all my fault—

"Hitoma."

Usami's ringing voice pulled me back to reality.

To a summer sky with the clouds high above and the sun just starting to set.

To the hot, muggy after-school classroom.

To the voices of students playing in the yard coming from a distance.

And to the beautiful young girl standing in front of me, Usami.

Right. This isn't the same classroom.

I sucked in a deep breath and calmed myself down.

"Hitoma, let me ask you again." Usami fixed me with her gaze, not letting me look away. Proof of her committed intentions, maybe.

The student in front of me wasn't the student from that time. It was Usami.

Sui Usami, who craved good grades and who wanted to become human faster than everyone else.

That Usami slowly extended her hand to me.

"I need your help!"

Usami wanted time badly enough to break one of the school's most important rules, despite the effort she had been making to graduate this whole time.

The only teacher who could grant her wish, most likely, was me.

If I took Usami's hand, no doubt I would be severely punished along with her.

Even so.

"This might be your last chance to see her, right?" I asked.

Usami twitched.

If I took her hand.

If I didn't take her hand.

I considered my options.

Which should I pick?

Which decision would I regret the least?

This situation was different from before.

Usami had a clear goal and had come to me for help.

Even if she had to throw away everything she'd built at this school…
All for the single goal of going to the side of the person she was indebted to…

Yeah. It'll be okay.

"You've braced yourself for whatever lies ahead?" I asked.
"Of course," Usami replied firmly.

Good. In that case, let's go.
Let's run away from this school.
I took Usami's proffered hand.

* * *

I'll briefly explain Usami's and my plan.
First, Usami would disguise herself and hide her ears.
In order for my ring to work on her, we'd hold hands as we walked out of the barrier.
Then we'd go to the hospital where her owner, Seiko Kizaki, had been admitted.
We knew where she was hospitalized. The name of the hospital was written in the documents the principal had presented to us earlier about the exemption that had been afforded to Usami.
Usami appeared in front of me, wearing a hat pulled low over her eyes.
"Sorry to keep you waiting, Hitoma."
"Hey. That was fast. Was everything okay at the dorm?"
"I was careful. No one saw me."
"…Right."
Usami had gone back to the dorm to change. We'd chosen to meet up in the middle of the forest.
From our position, we could see the cherry blossom tree at the edge of the barrier in the distance.

"Um, so you'll have to hold my hand from this point on...," I said. "Can you not look so blatantly disgusted, though?"

Her withering stare was going to cause me to lose my nerve for reasons completely unrelated to our escape plan, and I wanted her to cut it out.

"*Sigh*... If I have to."

"What are you talking about...? We were holding hands back in the classroom earlier..."

"...The grip was different."

"True."

Fair enough.

We had gripped each other's hands only to shake them, which was different from what we had to do to leave. It would be a problem if our hands came apart, so we had decided earlier to interlace our fingers.

Usami released a small sigh and stuck out her hand.

"...Here."

It was difficult to take her hand for a variety of reasons.

Is this really okay?

In the corner of my mind, a voice whispered, *There could be better options.*

If I took her hand, there was nothing I could do but go forward.

There would be no turning back.

Usami must have sensed my indecision. With an irritated expression, she grabbed my hand roughly.

"Geez... How unreliable can you get?" she said exasperatedly and pulled me forward. She strode resolutely toward the barrier.

There was no uncertainty in her steps. She was focused single-mindedly on meeting with her benefactor. I had to work to keep up with her unusually fast pace.

We'd be passing the cherry blossom tree soon. Nearly at the edge of the barrier. Would we be able to cross?

Speaking from experience, the person wearing the ring—me—and everything touching me should be able to pass through the barrier. Every day, my clothes, my bag, and all the things I carried inside had come in and out with no problem.

But would that be the case for Usami?

We drew up next to the cherry blossom tree.

The time came for us to step outside the barrier.

I was right. The barrier made allowances for anything touching the wearer of the ring.

Usami and I both successfully made it past the barrier.

She looked the same as she did at school.

"…We did it," I said.

There really was no going back after this.

"Hitoma, don't you dare let go of my hand."

Usami's hand tightened around mine. It was quivering.

If I let go, she would no longer be able to maintain her current form and would return to being a regular bunny plushie.

Until she reentered the barrier, she wouldn't regain her appearance as the human Usami.

Me too—without the ring, I would forget all about Usami and this school.

We were in this together, come hell or high water.

We embarked on our great adventure, braced for the consequences ahead.

* * *

"Usami, Kenichi proposed to me. He said, 'Will you marry me?'"

Marry? That's the thing where you get to spend your life together, right? Wow!

"But I'm not sure…"

Why? You've always liked Ken! What's there to be unsure of?

"I…I'm not a suitable marriage candidate for his family…"

I don't know anything about his family… But I'll be happy as long as you find happiness, Seiko!

"I didn't think anything of it when we were in school, but Kenichi's

from a really prestigious and wealthy family. He even had a fiancée, but his sister told me I ruined their engagement plans..."

Is Ken's sister a bad person...? You look sad.

"Am I really good enough for him...?"

Nonsense. Of course you are! I'm sure Ken would say the same!

"Usami...let's sleep together today. It's been so long."

Really? Can we?! Yippee! It's been ages since I got to sleep with you!

"I wish I could have a real conversation with you, Usami..."

Me too. I wish I could tell you all the things I'm thinking about.

But I...I'm a stuffed animal.

You can hug me, but I can't hug you back.

I can feel your warmth, but I have none to give you.

Someday, if my wish could be granted...

I have so many things I want to share with you.

* * *

A little less than two hours had passed since we left the school's barrier.

The swaying of the bus rocked Usami and me back and forth.

To get to the hospital where Seiko Kizaki had been admitted, we had to take a bus, transfer to a train, and then ride a second bus for three stations.

Usami stared out at the passing scenery with curiosity.

According to my research, the hospital's visiting hours were until seven in the evening. We left the school around four, so Usami would have only around an hour to meet with Ms. Kizaki. For the sake of that one short hour, we were risking mucking up our futures.

It didn't seem worth it.

It wasn't worth it. But...the time we all had to spend with others, to talk with others, was much, much shorter than we imagined.

We pulled up to a bus stop.

"Next one?" Usami, with her hat pulled low to hide her bunny ears, asked in a muffled voice.

"The one after that," I replied quietly.

I wondered how the other passengers saw us.

Me and Usami.

A man of medium build nearing thirty with a cute, delicate young girl. Worst-case scenario, they would see a dad looking after his daughter...

Ack... I hope we can at least pass as siblings... But our faces look too different for that. Ugh, it hurts. I should stop thinking about it.

The bus stopped again.

"Next one?" Usami repeated, sounding more nervous than last time.

"Yeah." I kept my reply brief.

I gripped her hand tighter. Maybe her anxiety was contagious.

I hadn't held a girl's hand since elementary school... This wasn't the time for such intrusive thoughts, but when I considered the fact that there was a girl's hand in mine, I became nervous for an entirely different reason.

Usami's hand was small enough that I could envelop it fully with mine. It was ever so slightly warm.

Unaware of my particular brand of nervousness, Usami continued staring out the window.

Her eyes reflected in the glass were focused far out in the distance.

* * *

"Mommm, this stuffed animal's gotten pretty old. I know you've had it for ages, but isn't it about time we got rid of it?"

"Hmmmm..."

I might be an antique, but....Seiko gives me a bath regularly! I can keep going for years and years!

"Your cough hasn't stopped, either, has it, Mom? Stuffed animals are magnets for dust if you just leave them lying around. It's not good for your health."

What....? Seiko's health is getting worse because of me....?

"But Usami's been with me ever since I was a little girl, you know. I can't bear to part with her now."

Y-yeah! I've been with Seiko the longest out of anyone in this house! That's why—

"Listen, Mom, I admire the way you treasure your belongings, but hasn't it been long enough? Look, the bunny agrees with me. She's saying, 'It's time to say bye-bye now.'"

I didn't say anything of the sort! Don't put words in my mouth when you don't know the first thing about me!

"But..."

"Ugh, fine! Then at least let me put it somewhere out of sight. It's not like I'm throwing it away. I'm just worried about your health, Mom."

Why would you do that...? Just being by Seiko's side is enough for me. That alone is everything for me.

* * *

"It's here...apparently...," I said.

It was 6:03 PM. The September sky was still bright. Usami and I were standing in front of a large hospital.

"Are you all right, Usami?"

Usami, beside me, lacked her usual vigor. Her expression was stony.

"...I'm fine."

She was putting on a brave front and feigning calm, but there was a quaver in her voice.

It was understandable.

She was meeting with a person she hadn't had the chance to see the entire time she was at school. The reunion was all the more momentous because this person was the reason why Usami wanted to become human.

Incidentally, there had been a question eating at me since earlier.

"Usami..."

"Wh-what...?"

She seemed thrown off by my uncharacteristically serious demeanor, but she looked steadily back at me with an earnest expression.

I took a breath before I spoke again. Usami swallowed heavily.

"This building is massive. Where in the world do we enter?" I asked.

"Excuse me...?" She laughed helplessly. I sensed the tension drain from her body. "You're seriously an idiot, Hitoma."

* * *

Somehow, we managed to find the entrance. Inside the hospital, Usami and I filled out the forms needed to visit an inpatient.

Usami bought a few get-well treats at the hospital shop. In doing so, she demonstrated why she belonged in the advanced class. From her use of money to her interaction with the matronly clerk, she did everything perfectly. The beginner students had to be taught what money even was.

During her years as a human's plush toy, Usami must've had plenty of opportunities to learn about human culture.

The entire time she was making her purchase, we were, of course, holding hands. Our interlaced fingers earned us a dubious look from the clerk.

Indeed, my very presence was causing the other people to stare at us weirdly.

I finished up the forms and turned them in at the nurses' station. That was the end of my role in the play for now. Usami seemed to have been vaguely uneasy about riding public transport and filling out paperwork alone, but at this point, all that was left was for her to go to the sick room, and she didn't need me around for that.

I had been mulling this over since we left the school.

"Usami."

"What is it?"

What Usami required wasn't me but the ring around my finger.

"Can you go on by yourself?"

"Huh...?!"

My question had flustered her. Of course it had.

"It'll be easier for you to have a proper conversation with Ms. Kizaki without me around."

"Huh...? But what about the ring...?" she asked, squeezing my hand harder, perhaps worried that I was going to abandon her here.

"I'll lend it to you."

Usami's eyes widened when she heard my answer.

Without the ring, my memories of Usami, why I had come here, and the school itself would all disappear and be replaced by false ones.

However, that would only be temporary.

"Once I touch the ring again, I'll remember everything," I said. "But your situation is different."

Uncertainty swam in Usami's eyes, sensing what I wanted her to do.

"Are you telling me to go meet with Seiko by myself…?" she asked.

Exactly.

"You see, I was playing video games all night yesterday, and I'm getting pretty sleepy. You know how it is," I drawled. "You've dragged me all the way here. Can you blame a guy for wanting to rest a bit? It's not like I'm getting overtime pay. So…uh, yeah, I'm gonna chill on that sofa over there! In the meantime, go and chat it up with your friend!"

I had realized something about Usami in the months that I'd known her.

It was surprisingly easy to read what she was thinking.

Like the fact that she was still feeling guilty that she had made me accompany her, even though it wasn't as if she had had any other option. Or that she suspected I was lying about pulling an all-nighter. Or that she thought if I was telling the truth, it might actually be a good idea for me to take a break. But she felt uneasy carrying on alone. And because she was serious by nature, she would never consent to any drastic measures that couldn't be undone.

"Hmm," I said. "I don't think I'll be able to sleep soundly, so maybe I'll take some of my usual sleeping pills. Usami, once I fall asleep, take off my ring and put it on your own finger without letting go of my hand. Then go and see Ms. Kizaki. I'll be sleeping like a baby while you're gone."

"But…"

"Usami."

Usami was very bright. We had already come all the way here. She would've realized dithering was only a waste of time.

"…Okay," she agreed.

And so I slipped off into dreamland.
Good night, Usami.
I hope you have a good talk with Ms. Kizaki.

By the way, Usami might have thought I was lying out of kindness.
But I was, by nature, low-key garbage.
My all-nighter and extreme drowsiness were both very, very real.

* * *

"My dear Usami."
...?
"Long time no see."
Seiko...
"Sorry for leaving you all alone in a place like this."
Don't worry about it.
"Ha-ha, just seeing your face puts me at ease for some reason."
What's wrong?
"I never change, do I? Every time something happens, I run straight to you..."
Seiko?
"It's Kenichi—he passed away today."
Ken died?
"We're both in our seventies now. You could say he lived a full life, but... ever since he married me, he's been shunned by his family and has been fighting all his battles alone this whole time. He pushed himself too hard, and it took a toll on his health... Maybe he shouldn't have married me after all..."
That's not true. Trust me.
Ken looked happy whenever he was with you.
That's why I figured I could entrust him with you.
"My daughter will be moving out soon, and then I'll be all alone."
You're not alone. I'm here.

"What am I supposed to do from now on?"

Seiko...?

"I wish you were alive, Usami."

I...

"You're my precious best friend. If only you were human and we had been actual childhood friends."

I...I also wish I were human—like you.

I also wish I were alive—the same as you. I wish I could stay by your side.

* * *

The sky was dyed with the colors of twilight.

I wonder how many more times I'll get to see this sky.

My name is Seiko Kizaki. Seventy-six years old. My husband passed away four years ago. My only daughter is living abroad with a family of her own. I have few friends, and none who are close enough to visit me at the hospital after I was admitted.

I watched the twilight sun, debating whether I should turn on the light or not. It was about that time. At that moment, a knock at the door interrupted my contemplation. It was probably the nurse. But it wasn't dinnertime yet... I called out, "Yes?" to alert whoever was at the door that I was inside.

By way of response, the door slid open slowly, hesitantly.

There stood a lone girl, cute and dainty. She looked like she was in middle school.

I thought she was an angel.

She had a fair complexion and silky, lavender-colored hair. Her red eyes glittered like gems.

"Do you have the wrong room?" I asked her.

"N-no, this is the right place."

Her voice reminded me in some way of my own from long ago. Oh, but maybe that's rather conceited of me.

The young girl watched me. Perhaps it was my imagination, but I thought I saw her eyes glaze over with tears. Our eyes met, and she looked away, unsure. She tugged her hat down over her head. Her lips were pressed flat into a line like she was trying to hold something back.

Her expression was grave. However, I had never met this girl before. Oh—she was around the same age as my granddaughter, though their build was completely different.

"Could you be a friend of my granddaughter?" I asked.

"No."

Ah, so I was wrong. I had guessed my granddaughter, who was living overseas, had asked her friend to check up on me, but if I thought about it carefully, that would have been an odd request.

In that case, surely she had indeed mistaken me for someone else.

"I'm the only one staying in this room...," I informed her.

"I know. I came to meet with you, Seiko."

Seiko.

How long had it been since someone called me by my first name? My friends from back in the day all called me "Seiko," but I had lost contact with them. I didn't even know their numbers.

"Seiko..." The young girl called my name in a fragile but desperate voice. "...You might not believe me, but I'm Usami. I was always by your side as your...stuffed rabbit, Bunny."

* * *

Seiko.

I want to become human like you, Seiko.

Then I would be able to tell you how I feel.

When you're lonely, I can hug you tight.

That's why—

That's why I have to say good-bye for a while.

Actually, I want to stay with you always.

But if I can stand beside you as a human, I'll be able to do more for you.

Seiko, I'm sorry for disappearing all of a sudden.
Don't forget me.

I love you the most!

* * *

"Bunny...?"

As the young girl had said, Usami was the plush bunny I had cherished ever since I was a little girl. Admittedly, her nickname wasn't my most creative work. She was a rabbit, hence "Bunny." The stuffed animal was about the same size as a real rabbit and had short, light-purple fur.

But when my daughter had come back home two, three years ago, she threw Bunny away without consulting me...

I had been so overwrought by Bunny's disappearance that I had made an international call to my daughter to check. At the time, she had told me, "I didn't do anything of the sort..."

This girl claimed she was Bunny... What in the world was she talking about?

Bunny wouldn't be in a place like this. Besides, Bunny was a stuffed animal.

While I was struggling to understand the situation, the self-proclaimed "Usami" started to look increasingly upset, like she was about to cry.

"I'm sorry to spring this on you..."

Where had this girl learned about Bunny?

"...I know it's sudden and that you probably don't believe me." She took a bottle of Calpico from the plastic bag she was holding. "Um, as a present, erm, I brought you the drink you used to like. You said you drank it with Ken the first time you hung out together."

The girl's words brought back a memory from long ago. Ken was the nickname of my husband—he had crossed to the other side four years ago.

It was a memory from my middle-school days, back when neither Ken nor I knew much about each other. I had been ecstatic that we were going to be hanging out just the two of us for the first time, and had dressed to the nines. It was a day I had been looking forward to.

We had planned to see a movie, but the tickets were sold out, and we couldn't get into the theater. Instead, we decided to talk at a coffee shop.

The drink we ordered was...Calpico.

I had completely forgotten that until now.

Why did this girl know something I barely remembered?

She held out the bottle tentatively toward me.

...Was it okay for me to accept it?

The girl looked fragile. Her expression was a mixture of hopeful, uncertain, and just a tiny bit expectant, as if she was handing a crush a love letter for the first time in her life.

I didn't know what her motive was, but I took the bottle she offered me.

"...Thank you for visiting me," I told her, the words spilling out of me naturally as I accepted the drink.

I had a mountain of questions for the girl, but I was genuinely happy that she had come out of her way to see a lonely old woman like me.

The bottle sparkled in the light of the sinking sun. It was still cold. Had she just bought it?

The girl seemed somewhat relieved that I'd taken her present.

"Um, are you really Bunny...?" I asked.

The girl's gaze wavered briefly, as if she was unsure what my words meant. Then she clasped her hands tightly in front of her chest, her expression tense. Once again, it looked like she was restraining herself.

She slowly nodded. "...That's right." Her voice was blurred with tears. "I'm Bunny, the one who's been by your side for longer than anyone else."

The girl took a step forward. At the same time, her hat fell off her head.

When I saw what was underneath, I gulped.

Growing from the girl's head were long, fluffy rabbit ears. But that wasn't all.

Her hair clip... That hair clip was—

"That's the clip I gave Bunny..."

I'd made it myself. There was none other like it in the world.

I had tried my hand at resin art as a hobby in my old age.

My eyes didn't deceive me. The rabbit clip was slightly misshapen and dark pink—a hair clip suitable for a young girl. It was my first work of art and my present to Bunny.

I remembered. I remembered the day I had given the clip to her.

"...Four years ago, when Ken passed away, you were really depressed." The words tumbled awkwardly out of the girl's mouth—the girl with the long ears and rabbit clip she had accidentally revealed. "You were cleaning up Ken's room when you found a book and a letter. You read the letter and...cried. A lot."

The book had been an unfamiliar one. My husband wouldn't have been interested in something that sounded as chic as *A Primer to Resin Arts*. The letter accompanying it had been addressed to me. The envelope had a decorative cosmos flower printed on it, and the letter had been written on matching stationery.

My late husband's feelings had been penned across the page in a neat, precise hand.

I still remembered what he had written.

The young girl stroked the clip gently. "You made this for me following along with that book."

I had made it the very day I had found the book and letter.

The only ones who knew about the letter and the clip were Bunny and me.

If anyone else had been in the room, they would have thought I had developed dementia.

Or could it be that this girl was a hallucination visible only to me?

Or a dream that showed me what I wanted to see?

*   *   *

That's all right.
If this is a dream, it's a joyful one.
Isn't that right, Kenichi?
Now I have one more story to tell you when we reunite.
I know this girl standing before me.

"Bunny." I called her nickname softly. "To be honest, I didn't believe you… But you really are Usami, aren't you…? You really are Bunny."

The girl's red eyes opened wide in surprise. "Yeah, I am…"

Tears welled up in her eyes, and her youthful but refined features contorted.

A large tear slid down her cheek.

"…! I am…! Seiko…I wanted to see you so, so badly! I have…so many things to tell you…!" She kept her eyes on me, not bothering to wipe away the fat drops of tears spilling down one after another.

Without thinking, I found myself embracing the girl who was trying with all her might to express how she felt.

Her tears on my hand were warm, like I was.

"Seiko…! I'm sorry for disappearing out of nowhere…! But I wanted to become human to be together with you…! All this time, I wanted to tell you *I love you* and *thank you*…!"

I lightly stroked the sobbing girl's head.

With my husband gone and my daughter moved away, I had thought there was no one who cared about me. All that was left for me was to take my leave of this world.

However, I was wrong.

"Usami… Thanks for coming to see me." Warmth blossomed in my chest. "I've always loved you, too."

Alas, in my old age, I was easily moved to tears. Both our faces became messy with tears. It was kind of funny.

"Ha-ha, we must look horrible," I said.

"No way. Seiko is cute and pretty no matter what," Usami protested.

We looked at each other and broke out giggling at the same time.

When was the last time someone had called me cute? I felt as if I was a young girl again, if only on the inside.

The reason was surely the love this girl…no, Usami had for me.

The two of us started to gossip about the years we had been apart, just like old friends from the same all-girls school.

* * *

"You must be studying hard at your school."

"I am! But graduating this year…might be difficult. I'll definitely graduate next year and become human! Then I'll live together with you, Seiko!"

Usami had been studying furiously and working herself to the bone to accomplish her goal of living with me.

She was determined.

Determined, focused, her gaze trained directly on her dream of a happy future with me.

In that case, I had to tell her.

"Usami," I said in a gentle, quiet voice. I smiled slightly so as not to scare her.

She pursed her lips, perhaps sensing the serious nature of what I was about to tell her.

Usami, I'm sorry this is the news I have to tell you.

"I…I was told that I only have one more month to live."

Usami's ears leaped up. Her expression was grim.

I had only been informed of my prognosis in the afternoon the day before. I had steeled myself the day I had fallen, but it was tough to say the words myself.

"That's why I can't live with you, Usami."

She was silent, not saying a word.

I took her lovely, doll-like hand with my thoroughly wrinkled ones.

Nostalgia welled up inside me when I touched her. It was strange. She should have felt completely different from her stuffed-animal self.

Usami's eyes were glassy with tears. I wondered if she hadn't said anything because there was nothing she could say. Or was it because she was in the process of choosing carefully what to say?

Sorry, Usami. I'm sorry to make you sad.

Her mouth moved minutely. "I don't...want that..."

"I know. I wanted to live together, too." I did my best to speak to her calmly.

"If you're not here, everything I've worked for will have been for nothing..."

"Sorry. But I don't think your effort is meaningless."

"It is...! I persevered this whole time for your sake...!" she protested while sobbing. "...! I shouldn't have tried to become human... I should have stayed by your side the whole time...!"

"Don't say something so sad." I gently petted her. She kept her face turned down. "Do you like humans, Usami?"

"I like you, Seiko." Her reply was instant.

"I know. Thanks... You know, a lot has happened in my life, but at the end of the day, I like humans."

"...There's a lot of awful ones."

"That's true. But I still like them."

"You don't like stuffed animals?"

"No, I do."

"...You like everything, then. That's cheap." Usami puffed up her cheeks. She was adorable even when she was pouting.

"What do you like other than me?"

Usami pondered my question. "...School, I guess. I don't hate it. And learning. It's fun to find out things I don't know." Then a gentle smile rose to her face. "...I don't hate humans, either."

That must mean that her school was a healthy environment. Thank goodness. She had a place she belonged other than at my side.

"Is there anything you want to do in the future?" I asked.

"I'm not sure. But..." Usami squeezed my hand tight and raised her head to look at me. "...I think it would be nice if I could help people like you who are sick. That way, there would be fewer people who had to experience painful things like you and I have...! So...that's why, in the future, I want to be a doctor...!" she declared. Within her red eyes burned a bright fire.

Usami was a strong child. Smart. Thoughtful.

"I see. I think that's wonderful."

It was possible, even, that she had said what she had only so as not to worry me.

I hugged her tightly.

Please. Please—

"I love you, Usami."

Please let Usami be happy even after I'm gone.

An unfeeling, mechanical chime rang through the hospital.

Visiting hours were over.

I released Usami from my embrace.

"By the way, did you come here by yourself?" I asked.

From her stories, her school seemed to be strict in some respects, but it apparently hadn't been a problem for her to come here.

"Oh, um...I came with my teacher. But Hito—I mean, Mr. Hitoma left us alone out of consideration."

So that's how it is.

It was going to get dark soon. I had been worried about her return journey, but I could rest easy knowing her teacher was accompanying her.

"What a kind teacher."

"...I guess. He's a little unreliable, but...he's not a bad guy."

Oho?

Seeing Usami turned bashful, a part of me wanted to bully her just a little.

"...Sounds like someone has a teensy crush on her teacher. Am I right?"

"What?! How did the conversation end up here?"

"What do you mean? Haven't I always come to you with stories about romance?"

"You're not wrong… Ken was all you ever talked about…"

"See? So? How are things between you?"

"I-it's completely impossible! You're my number one, Seiko!"

"Oh? Are you *suuure* it's impossible?"

"Knock it off! Stop teasing me!"

I was having so much fun joking around with Usami that I found myself wishing time would stop.

But that was one wish that couldn't be granted.

The door to my sickroom opened.

A nurse entered and said, "I've brought your dinner, Ms. Kizaki."

Hidden in the shadow of the curtain, Usami scrambled to put her hat back on.

"Oh my! Is this your granddaughter? You're such a lovely little lady! But I'm afraid visiting hours are already over."

"Ah, I-I'm sorry," Usami stuttered, stepping away from my bedside.

Wait. I'm not ready—

"Wai—" I choked down my words and hurriedly withdrew the hand I had instinctively reached out, reluctant to say farewell.

Why did I do that? That's only going to upset her.

Usami glanced at me. It looked like she was going to cry.

But in the next moment, she smiled warmly.

"Seiko."

She turned around and looked straight at me.

This was good-bye.

I sensed from her expression that this was the last chance I would be able to speak with her properly.

We really were going to part ways.

This was truly the last time. I didn't want to miss a single one of Usami's words or expressions.

Usami slowly opened her mouth.

* * *

"Thank you for treasuring me."

She turned a brilliant smile on me, beaming from ear to ear.

"I'll love you forever and always!"

* * *

"Mr. Hitoma."

A voice broke through my dozing.

Who…?

"Thanks. I got to talk to Seiko."

The dainty voice was that of a young girl.

I didn't recognize it.

"I'm going to become human. I promised Seiko."

Seiko…?

Nothing this person said made sense to me.

Plus, I was still sleepy. I didn't want to think about anything.

Man, waking up always puts me in a bad mood. Let me sleep to my heart's content.

"Mr. Hitoma."

…Could she be talking to me? No, I'm sure I'm just being overly self-conscious.

"I planned to live solely for Seiko's sake. But I was wrong. She wouldn't want that."

What is this, a budget romance novel…? Not that I'm one to talk. At least she sounds happy.

"I figured out my dream for the future, and I want you to hear it. I'm going to help humans. I'm going to be a doctor. I know it'll be tough, but I'll do my best. I want to give people more time with the ones they love."

Oh yeah? But it's hard to become a doctor. Not that I'm an expert on the details. It's not as if I've ever been tasked with being a career adviser.

"I wanted to say thanks. I discovered what I want to do because you

took me here. You taught me something valuable. Even if I can't make my dream come true, I can find another one. My efforts haven't been worthless. They make up the path I take and my experiences."

I didn't know who she was thanking, but I was happy to see even a single student find their path in life.

Life is long. Depending on your choices, you might be surprised to find that you can change your life again and again. Just kidding. I guess that's too optimistic. Nevertheless, there isn't just one path to happiness.

I'm so sleepy. It's about time for my brain to shut down.

The girlish, doll-like voice was still droning, but it couldn't win against my drowsiness.

Sorry, dolly. I don't dislike your voice. Let me listen to your stories some other time.

Cocooned in the fluffy and warm atmosphere, I drifted off again.

* * *

"WAKE. UP!!!"

"AGHHH!!!"

Startled by the loud shout straight in my ear, I flew out of my seat.

Who? What? Huh? What's going on…?!

More importantly, what's on top of me…?

"…Did you forget you have to keep holding my hand?"

I was lying on the ground, having fallen from the chair, and hovering above me on all fours was Usami with a fed-up expression.

Wh-wh-wh-what is she doing…?! This makes it look like she pushed me down with our hands clasped together…!

"We have to leave or we're going to get kicked out of the hospital soon, Hitoma. This is all your fault. You sure took your time waking up."

What's that? Hospital? …Oh! Right, I remember now!!

I rebooted my half-asleep brain.

That was right. Usami and I had snuck out of the school and come to the hospital to meet with Usami's benefactor, Seiko Kizaki.

I glanced at our connected hands to see my ring on Usami's hand.

We sat up.

"Were you able to talk with Seiko?" I said to her, wondering how much to ask.

Usami's lips curved in a soft, gentle smile, as if my question had prompted her to remember their conversation.

"Yeah, we talked," she answered. I didn't know why, but she seemed a little more mature than she had before we had come.

"Okay. That's good."

To be honest, I was worried this experience would only hurt her further, but it appeared that my fears had been groundless.

I was sure they had a good conversation.

Usami's expression was far brighter than it had been earlier.

"Forget that! Like I said, we have to go! Time to go back!"

"All right, all right."

Usami pulled me to the exit.

Unauthorized leave of campus, contact with outside humans, and most likely violation of dorm curfew.

We had stacked up several rule infractions in one day and were sure to be punished once we returned to the school.

But strangely, I didn't regret a thing.

We exited the hospital to find that the sun had set. The moon and stars shone in the sky.

The wind was cool.

The summer seemed endless.

But it, too, had an end.

Together, Usami and I walked to the bus stop in front of the hospital.

Come on. Let's go back to school.

* * *

One week and one day passed.

I was in the math prep room before classes started, bathing in the golden glow of the autumn sun and sipping on a cup of Mr. Hoshino's first-rate coffee.

"Geez, you sure had it rough, Mr. Hitoma," he said to me nonchalantly.

"Yeah, but I got what was coming to me."

It had been eight days since Usami's and my escape. Upon returning to campus from meeting with Usami's benefactor, we were taken immediately to the principal's office and lectured by the principal until our ears fell off. The man might resemble a mascot character, but he was terrifying when he was angry.

Usami and I had been given the following punishments.

Rei Hitoma: three-month salary reduction.

Sui Usami: one-week suspension plus a 150-point deduction out of her points needed to become human.

The salary reduction was a serious bummer, but I felt lucky it wasn't anything worse.

In the worst-case scenario, there had been a better-than-good chance of me losing my job. For Usami, expulsion hadn't been out of the question, either. The punishments meted out were lenient in comparison. Apparently, the decision had been made at the director's discretion.

"How long is Usami suspended?" Mr. Hoshino asked me.

"Yesterday. She's coming back to school today."

Usami's sudden suspension had thrown the rest of the students for a loop.

The reason why had yet to spread around the school. In my position, I was obligated to deny all rumors regardless of whether they were accurate or not. Usami was unlikely to admit anything herself, either.

"Oh, look at the time. We should head back to the teachers' office soon," Mr. Hoshino pointed out, and we did just that.

I wasn't a morning person at all, but with a cup of Mr. Hoshino's coffee in my system, the fog in my brain had cleared slightly. Must've been a wake-up blend.

* * *

We passed by the main entrance on our way from the prep room on the first floor to the teachers' office. I couldn't avoid seeing the bottles labeled with the students' names even if I tried. The contents of the bottles were hidden. Usami's bottle was lined up with the rest.

The 150-point deduction from her punishment had emptied her bottle completely. Her prospects of graduating this year were grim.

"Oh, Hitoma. Morning."

"Ack—?! Oh, uh, m-morning," I stammered.

Speak of the devil.

"What the…? You're acting sus. It's creepy."

Scathing as always.

I'd been surprised only because she showed up right when I was thinking about her.

"Ah, Usami. Good morning," Mr. Hoshino said.

"Long time no see, Mr. Hoshino. Good morning."

"You call *him* 'Mister.' Why not me?" I protested.

"There's no reason to," said Usami. "'Hitoma' is good enough."

That's discrimination… The one time she called me "Mr. Hitoma" might have been a miracle.

"Please help me convince her, Mr. Hoshino."

"Hmm, I don't know. We value the students' independence here."

"Don't go crying to Daddy, Hitoma," Usami drawled. "It's pathetic."

"You… What's more important, your independence or your manners?" I demanded.

"That's my decision to make."

"Ugh… I feel like you're just arguing with me for the sake of it… Anyway, the two of you sure are chummy…"

Mr. Hoshino made a small noise and looked skyward like he had just recalled something. "Maybe it's because I was her homeroom teacher until last year? The teacher in charge of the intermediate class is me, remember?"

"Mr. Hoshino's classes are easy to understand. He's a good teacher," Usami said.

Wow, is that a diss against my classes?

"I'm going up to the classroom," Usami added. "Bye, Mr. Hoshino. See ya, Hitoma."

"See you in a bit," I said.

She walked off in the direction opposite of the way we were going. Her retreating footsteps sounded more buoyant than they had before.

And so, my run-of-the-mill days with the four advanced students resumed once more.

The Misanthrope and
Tobari's Hymn

I like beautiful things.

I like beautiful sounds.

Humans must see the same landscape I do. The same but different.

Will I be able to see it, too?

Will I be able to find beautiful things in this world?

* * *

Ugh…I'm screwed.

This is the worst… Ahhhh… What have I done…?

"Whoa. Mr. Hitoma? What are you doing?"

"Ack—! Haneda?! That's my question! It's late!"

Classes were already over. Haneda had caught me slumped over the podium with my head buried in my hands. I scrambled to stuff the object on the table into my pocket.

"…Hey, what did you hide just now?" Haneda asked.

Why does she look so amused…?

She sauntered up to me, a mischievous glint in her eyes.

Not good, not good, not good, not good!

I have no choice. There's only one thing to do at a time like this…!

"Oh my god! An alien! Over there, in the sky!" I shouted.

"…Huh?"

What on earth is wrong with me?

Why did I say that?

I could've come up with a way better tactic than that.

"Wow, you're a terrible liar... Besides, the door was open. I saw it before I came in. Your secret."

...Is she bluffing now?

What do I do...? She has me at a slight disadvantage. Hmm...Guess I'll feign ignorance.

"...What are you talking about?" I asked cautiously.

"The grimy, fancy handkerchief you hid just now."

"You seriously saw it?!"

"Say, isn't that Mr. Hoshino's?"

She sure did get a clear look...

"Ugh, fine, I surrender. Yeah, you're right... It was an accident..."

Usually, whenever I was down in the dumps or I'd messed up, I went to Mr. Hoshino for advice. That wasn't an option this time. That was because the victim of my crime was Mr. Hoshino himself.

God, seriously... I'm such an idiot. Your textbook case of human trash, unfit for society...

Glum, I took the handkerchief I had tried to conceal out of my pocket and spread it over the podium to show Haneda.

"Look at this..."

On the fabric was a large brown splotch.

"What made this stain?" Haneda asked.

"Soy sauce."

"In what situation would you have spilled soy sauce here at school?"

Excellent question.

"Well...today is payday, you see. I was on a high and treated myself to sushi for lunch. However, I ended up not having enough time to eat, and it's too much of a hassle to take it home, so after school, when I was in the teachers' office, I decided to eat it."

"Gotcha. I'm starting to see what happened."

"Then I accidentally knocked over the soy sauce. I grabbed a nearby cloth and scrambled to wipe it up."

"And that cloth was Mr. Hoshino's handkerchief."

"Yeah..."

I looked at the handkerchief lying unfolded in front of me, wrestling with the reality of what I had done. I hung my head in shame.

My desk was next to Mr. Hoshino's in the teachers' office. Since I had started only this year, I didn't have many things on my desk.

But Mr. Hoshino was different.

His belongings were strewn across his desk and stacked in towers.

He was considerate enough to make sure that none of it spilled over into my space, but nonetheless, once in a while, one of the piles would lose the fight against gravity and come collapsing down onto my desk. It didn't bother me, really. Whenever it happened, I just restacked his documents and things without comment, usually musing to myself about how rough Mr. Hoshino had it.

Such was the setting where this tragedy took place.

Indeed, as you may have guessed, in a stroke of misfortune, Mr. Hoshino's handkerchief had ended up on my desk.

The cloth I had used to wipe up the spilled soy sauce had been on *my desk*.

The woeful hanky was a tragic by-product of his penchant for disorder and my carelessness.

"Look, shouldn't you hurry up and apologize to Mr. Hoshino already?" Haneda said in a blasé tone. She was leaning over the podium with her head propped in her hands.

"That's true… But before I do, I want to get it as clean as I can so I can return it."

When I had noticed what the cloth I'd used to wipe the mess actually was, I rinsed it right away. I had also tried a method I remember seeing on the internet, the idea of which was to press the stain with a damp cloth to transfer it…? I hadn't remembered the details clearly, but I'd attempted it anyway…

Still, I hadn't been able to remove the splotch entirely. Soy sauce was a tough opponent…

"Yeah? But there's no point in sequestering yourself and agonizing alone, is there? I'll go bring Mr. Hoshino for you."

"Idiot—! W-wait, Haneda!" I cried.

But Haneda skipped out of the classroom without heeding my words.

How did I get myself into this mess…?! I'm not ready yet…!

"Here he is," Haneda announced, returning to the room with Mr. Hoshino mere seconds after she had left.

"How fast were you running?!"

Did she just teleport?!

Mr. Hoshino's handkerchief, thoroughly dirtied with soy sauce, was still spread over the podium.

"Hng? What? What is it?" Mr. Hoshino asked, peering between Haneda and me.

Did she bring him without telling him anything?

And then:

"Oh, that's the brand-name handkerchief my wife bought me as a birthday present."

A-a-a-a birthday present from his wife?! From a high-end brand at that?!

It's not just expensive but has sentimental value, too?!

And did he say, "Wife"?! He's married?

Because of the handkerchief's quality, it had occurred to me that it was a present. There was no doubt that it was a cherished belonging!

I'm literally the worst…! What in the world have I done…?! I deserve to die—

"Yeesh, I thought I lost it," Mr. Hoshino said. "I didn't know what to do. Thanks. Where did you find it?" He flashed me a friendly smile and approached my podium.

Huh…? Did he miss the stain…?

"…Um, Mr. Hoshino, I'll explain. Your handkerchief was lying on my desk in the teachers' office, and I carelessly used it to wipe up some soy sauce… I'm really sorry…," I said, shrinking in on myself.

He cocked his head and parroted, "Soy sauce?" Then he picked up the cloth and inspected it closely. "Oh… Are you talking about this? Well, a stain of this degree is no big deal. I can still use it as intended. Don't worry about it, Mr. Hitoma." He folded it up roughly and put it into his pocket. "Anyway, I'm so relieved you found it. I've been looking for it for a whole week. I was ready to get an earful from my wife. Ah, Haneda, could this be the matter you wanted me for?"

"Mm-hmm."

"Gotcha. Thank you both." He bowed slightly and ambled out of the classroom.

He didn't mind that I had stained the handkerchief even though it was a precious gift...

I thought he would scold me or be sadder...

"Good thing he wasn't angry with you, right, Mr. Hitoma?"

Haneda was standing by the door, chuckling.

To be honest, she might have saved my skin.

At the rate I'd been going, I would've tortured myself with guilt all night and gone begging for mercy on my hands and knees in the morning.

"Yeah, thanks, Haneda."

She smiled in satisfaction and excused herself before exiting the room.

Tobari Haneda.

Originally from the avian family. A bull-headed shrike, to be precise. Her grades were number one. She was unquestionably the top of the class. Her tenure at the school was a secret. Also a mystery was how long she had been in the advanced class. Such information tended to be vague when it came to students who had been enrolled a long time. There were students with similar academic histories in the other classes, apparently. Haneda wanted to become human so that she could play music.

She had the best grades in the school, and with her approach toward life, she would easily adapt to human society.

Out of all the students, she was the closest to graduating.

Yet she remained in the advanced class year after year.

That was the Tobari Haneda I knew.

* * *

A few days later, a problem arose during my sixth-period history class.

"Sorry, Mr. Hitoma, but can I go to the nurse's office? My stomach hurts..."

It was Haneda. Her face was pale.

"Your stomach hurts?" I asked. "Are you okay? Do you need someone to go with you?"

"No, it's all right. I can go by myself." She turned down the offer of an escort even though it was visibly obvious to anyone that she was unwell. "Sorry to interrupt the class," she added.

"I don't want you falling on your way there. Take someone with you."

Usami's hand sprang up. "I'll go!" she volunteered.

That was rare. What a change from her usual grumbling about this and that being a waste of time and from her usual pissy expression.

"Okay. I'm counting on you, Usami."

The slight-framed Usami walked over to Haneda.

"No, really, I can go alone," Haneda insisted.

Usami shot down Haneda's rejection with her classic acerbity. "You're obviously sick, so you should just keep your lips zipped."

"Geez, I didn't take you for that kind of person," Haneda said. "Aren't classes your top priority?"

"You may be ill, but I see your mouth is as lively as ever. Hurry up and go take a nap in the nurse's office already," Usami said, dragging a woozy Haneda off with her to see the nurse.

It was just Minazuki, Oogami, and me in the classroom.

"I hope Haneda's okay...," Oogami said.

"With our constitutions, we almost never catch colds or get sick, so it's worrying," Minazuki remarked.

"Wow, really?" I said. "I'm jealous. I wish I didn't catch colds."

"Oh, that's not exactly it. It's just that our bodies are basically those of healthy teenage humans, so our immune systems are accordingly robust," Oogami explained.

I see.

The immune system of a healthy teenager... That was a sore point for someone nearing his thirties... Lately, even if I didn't end up with a full-blown cold, there were still times when my body felt heavy… I swallowed my bitterness quietly and resumed class.

I wondered if Haneda was all right. I resolved to check in on her once class was over.

* * *

The nurse's office.

It was already November. In the nearly eight months since I came to this school, I had yet to set foot in here.

The nurse's office—located on the first floor, right by the main entrance—felt like both a part of the school and not at the same time. The strange duality made me nervous.

I stood in front of the door and knocked lightly. Someone from inside immediately said, "Come in." It wasn't Haneda's voice, so it was likely the nurse.

I slid the door open slowly.

"…Excuse me. I'm Haneda's homeroom teacher. How's she doing?"

I stepped into the room, my curiosity making my actions more careful and deliberate.

The room was a run-of-the-mill nurse's office in every way. The staple medicinal scent filled the air. Instruments to measure height and weight were arranged around the room.

On the bulletin board was a newsletter with the latest health-related information. The cupboard was stocked with bandages, disinfectants, and other first aid items. Next to the door was a small two-seater sofa, where students were intended to sit, perhaps?

The school nurse was sitting at a desk set farther into the room.

If I remembered correctly, her name was Haruka Karasuma. Her black hair was styled in a wolf cut. She had a straight and slim figure. Large, black-rimmed glasses sat on her nose. She was a woman, but she was much more handsome than someone like me. Your classic cool beauty.

She looked younger than I was… Maybe the same age as Ms. Saotome or slightly younger? However, I couldn't say for sure. The most surprising thing about her was that she was—wait for it—a blood relative of our round, jolly principal.

"Hey, Mr. Hitoma. Wassup?" she said. "Ms. Haneda felt better after a quick cat nap."

"Good. Glad to hear it."

That was a relief.

Haneda was the student who had snapped up first place in the blink of an eye. No doubt she was working hard where no one could see her. It wasn't so strange to think that she had worn herself out.

"Seriously, can you talk to her?" Ms. Karasuma pleaded. "She gets sick every year around this time, and she never comes to see me until she's hanging on by a thread. Tell her to come in earlier next time, won't you? That or get some actual rest."

Every year?

"Does she have some sort of preexisting condition?" I asked.

Her face contorted as if struck by a realization, and she averted her gaze.

"Oh, ummm… Whoops. Anyway, you know how it is, right…?"

…I was curious to know what she was talking about, but everyone has their own circumstances.

The curtain partitioning the nurse's office rustled. There must have been a bed behind it.

"Mr. Hitoma?"

The curtain parted slightly to reveal Haneda, who looked like she had just woken up.

Her blouse wasn't buttoned as high as usual, and I was a little troubled over where to look.

"You came just to check on me?"

Her voice was softer and airier than usual. Was that because she had been sleeping until a second ago? Or was it because she hadn't fully recovered yet?

"How are you feeling?" I asked.

"Much better. Thanks for asking. How was the rest of class?"

"We covered up to page 124. Once you've regained your energy, drop by the teachers' office or social studies prep room, and I'll go over what you missed."

"What about the math prep room?"

"That's Mr. Hoshino's private sanctuary, so it's off-limits."

Haneda laughed cheerfully. "Ha-ha, that's so petty."

Come to think of it, I'd never had a chance to talk with Haneda at length... The last time we chatted was... Oh, right—during the handkerchief incident.

"Haneda," I said.

"Hmm? What?"

"Is there any music you have been into recently?"

Startled by the sudden question, Haneda looked at me with a guileless expression like a toddler's.

"...Pfft... Ah-ha-ha! What do you remind me of? You're like, you know, a dad worried about his daughter who's hit puberty."

D... D-dad... Her description wasn't inaccurate, but...

The nurse was smirking in our direction, too.

Stay in your lane...

"Ah-ha-ha! I haven't had this much fun in a while. Hmm...music I like lately. Oh, it might not be quite what you're asking, but I'm pretty into otoMAD vids recently. They always blow my expectations out of the water. I keep up with what's trending, but I watch a lot of older content as well."

OtoMAD—a popular type of mash-up videos.

Didn't expect that one. That sure takes me back. Frankly, had she said classical or western pop, I would've been stumped. This is much more my area of expertise. Actually, it's practically my home field. Why? Because I'm a nerd! I even own copies of video game soundtracks. On top of that—

"By the way, the song I'm obsessed with right now is 'Rumor Has It Chicken L*ttle Scored a Chicken Dinner.'"

That was one of my works.

It was a fevered track I had banged out in eight hours on one of my days off. You guessed it: My secret hobby was making otoMAD videos.

"I'm a low-key fan of this person's vids. Look. His username is Hitoman. It's kind of similar to your name, huh? Pretty funny."

I might be in trouble.

Did she already realize...?! Does she know I'm Hitoman...?!

"While you're here, want to watch? I'll show you one of his videos," she offered.

"No, I'm good."

Haneda ignored my response point-blank. "Good? Great. Then I'll play 'Rumor Has It Chicken L*ttle Scored a Chicken Dinner' for you."

From her phone came blaring a colorless backing track accompanied by rhythmical gunshots.

"His tracks have such groove. That's why I like them."

"O-oh?"

Darn it. That makes me kinda happy.

"Don't you write any music?" I asked.

"Hmm, once in a while for fun." She looked up from the screen and hit me with a bright smile. "Just like Mr. Hitoman."

"Wha—?!"

This sly little...! She knew everything from the start...!

"Hellooo," the nurse said, peeking in from a corner of the bed. "If you're feeling better, you should leave already."

"Oh, uh, okay," Haneda replied awkwardly.

Admittedly, holding a video screening in the nurse's office had been pushing it a little too far. The nurse gave us a soft warning.

We paused the video and got ourselves ready to leave.

"Do you think you're okay to go back?" I asked Haneda as she raised herself up.

"Yeah," she said. "I'm all right now." She stretched from her fingertips to her toes.

She certainly didn't look ill anymore. She slipped on her shoes and stood up from the bed. We said bye to the nurse and exited the room, and together we returned to the classroom where Haneda's belongings were.

"Hey, shouldn't you have brought me my stuff?" she asked. "Isn't that just good manners in situations like this?"

"No. I'm too scared to touch a female student's belongings."

"Just as well. You might be accused of sexual harassment if you're unlucky."

"Right?"

The truth was that it hadn't even occurred to me to bring her belongings to her... I was blindsided by my own inattentiveness.

No, I shouldn't do anything unnecessary.

I thought of the incident at my previous school, and my heart grew heavy. In the episode involving Usami a while ago, I had compromised too much, even if, ultimately, it had ended up well. It was better for me not to involve myself too deeply with the students.

There was no one left in the classroom. The other students had already gone home.

Haneda went to her seat. She packed her notebooks and textbooks into her bag.

She gets to go home. Must be nice.

I had a pile of year-end tasks waiting for me, and I had to prepare for exams and class.

"...Ahhh, I want to go home, too," I grumbled.

"Is that something you should say in front of a student?"

"There's nothing wrong with saying, 'I want to go home' when I want to go home. Take note. Don't work yourself too hard. You were helping Usami with her studies the other day, too, weren't you?"

"How did you know?!"

"Wa-ha-ha. Because I'm your teacher."

I acted big, but actually, I had just happened to see them holding a study session in the library.

Haneda was good at her studies and a good teacher. She was so good that sometimes I thought she could take my job if I let down my guard.

"I was talking with the other teachers, and they said that Usami's quiz scores have improved across the board."

"It's no biggie. It's natural to want to root for someone trying their best, you know. I'm not pushing myself too hard, either. Don't worry.

Besides that, I didn't realize you were watching me so closely. Though I'm not one to talk. I'm watching you right back... Did you know, you usually look super mellow, but sometimes a cloud comes over your face, and you get this look as if you're staring at something far away?"

"Huh, are you sure...?"

I hadn't realized.

"Yeah, like right after we finished talking in the hallway earlier... Oh, did I step on a land mine? My bad if I did."

"No, it's—"

—*nothing like that.*

I wanted to say it, but I couldn't. How could such a simple remark be a land mine? Yet memories of the past came flooding back.

When I didn't continue, Haneda said with concern, "Mr. Hitoma? Did I actually misstep? If something happened, I'll listen. And, you know, if you tell me about it, I won't make the same mistake again."

"No, it's all right. It looks like I made you worry. I'm sorry. It's... behind me..."

"But it isn't, is it? It's not squarely in the past. Isn't that why you find yourself thinking about it once in a while? You will feel lighter if you talk about it, I think."

Was that true...? Maybe it was.

But if it were in the past, if I were to put it in the past like Haneda said, I—

"You're making a scary face again, Mr. Hitoma." Haneda was peering at my expression. I had looked down without realizing it. "It's A-OK. Whatever happens, I'm here for you." She smiled.

Suddenly, I felt like crying.

The wound wouldn't disappear. I had run. I had averted my eyes, but even so, it was still there.

There was someone I had failed to protect. It was my fault.

I had wanted to be kind, to show that I cared, but I had failed.

It had been my mistake, so—

"Is it all right for me to put down this weight?"

"Why not?" Haneda answered easily. "The past will bear it for you. That's what I believe." Her voice was soft as the autumnal sun, but I sensed a strength deep within.

She looked at me tenderly.

Hiding in those eyes was the faintest hint of shadow. Was that just my imagination?

Maybe Haneda had a burden she had yet to give up to the past, too.

I didn't know Haneda very well yet. But that was surely the same for Haneda.

In that case, I'd be the first to share my wound.

It was the story of how I'd left my previous school.

My lips and tongue felt heavy as I slowly opened my mouth and said, "To tell the truth, I—"

"Mm-hmm," Haneda murmured encouragingly.

"At my previous school, one of my students came to me for advice. They were fighting with their friend. I was their homeroom teacher, so I wanted to help—but that was a mistake. Teachers are in a different position from students. In the end, because of me—because of my unnecessary words and actions—what started as a squabble snowballed, and the student who sought my help ended up quitting school. And when they left, for some reason, they lied that I had inflicted corporal punishment on them. I remember no such thing. I discussed everything with the school, but no one would listen—that's why I ended up quitting."

The story flooded out of me like a dam had broken. Haneda listened to it all.

"On my last day, coincidentally, I had a chance to talk with that very student. What do you think they said to me?"

"…What?"

"'It's all your fault. I just wanted to vent, but you took everything too seriously. It's your fault for trying to do something you couldn't. Serves you right.'"

The scene was still fresh in my mind.

It had been winter. In the biting chill of the classroom, the student screamed at me in tears.

"They were right. I was the one in the wrong. That's why—"

That's why it hurts.

It wasn't anyone else's fault but mine. I couldn't shift the blame onto anyone else. This whole time, this whole time—

—I've hated humans.

But the one I actually hated was myself.

Haneda listened to my story without interrupting. She had fallen silent and was looking down. Maybe she was troubled over how to respond.

I knew it. I shouldn't have said anything.

Finally, she said, "Mr. Hitoma, time marches on." She stated the obvious fact as if it were special wisdom.

"What...?"

"It's true that your past self will stick with you, but the one I'm looking at is the current you, so...it's okay. Even if you make a mistake, you can redo it over and over again." Her voice was filled with affection. "It's okay—I see you. The current you." She smiled softly.

"...Thanks."

"That's my line! Thanks for coming to this school, Mr. Hitoma!"

* * *

I finished telling my story. Right as I was thinking we should leave the classroom, Haneda said, "Say, Mr. Hitoma. You said you want to go home already, right?"

"Huh...?"

Where'd that come from...?

She clasped her hands behind her, taking one step closer to me, then another and another, peering up at me through her lashes.

Her prowling approach made me uneasy, and I backed away without thinking.

H-Haneda?

Aren't you a little too close…?

I found myself with my back up against the wall. Haneda's hand shot out and slammed into the wall next to my face with a *thud.*

Did I—did I seriously just get pinned against the wall…?!

"Uh…Haneda? Ma'am…?"

With Haneda right up in my face, the honorific slipped out of me unconsciously.

How did we end up here? I have no clue…!

Pleased at my reaction, Haneda smirked like the cat that had gotten the cream. "Mr. Hitoma, I'll bring out your true self."

Then she whispered in my ear.

"C'mon. Let's get out of here."

* * *

"Mm, the air is so refreshing!" Haneda exclaimed. "How long do you plan to stay by the door, Mr. Hitoma? Come with me."

"Um, are we really allowed here?!"

Earlier, when Haneda had whispered to me her invitation, I had braced myself to be propositioned with an off-campus getaway in a repeat of what had happened with Usami, but the place she brought me to was the school roof.

"I can't believe the door to the roof isn't locked… I had no clue…," I said.

I had thought unrestricted access to the roof was a privilege found only in fiction.

"Oh, no, it's usually locked. Students aren't allowed up here."

"So you're not supposed to be here!"

We're violating school rules!

I was panicking, but Haneda showed no sign of shame, letting the cool breeze wash over her, detached from the world.

This girl… How bold can you be…?

"That's weird. Then why was it open?" I asked.

If the door was left unlocked due to a teacher's or staff member's oversight, I might be able to overlook Hane—

"Ah, yes, let me explain!" She dug through her pocket with a twinkle in her eye. "I used this! I just have to tinker with the lock a little, and it pops right open. Piece of cake! I come up here all the time."

What she took out of her pocket was a small orange feather, most likely her own. Bathed in the light of the evening sun, it seemed to sparkle.

But more importantly...

"Lock picking...? Really?" I said.

Tobari Haneda. A force to be reckoned with...

The honor student at the top of the class with graduation in the bag was, in fact, an incorrigible delinquent.

I could no longer defend her rooftop break-in...

I had wondered why Haneda was still at this school despite how brilliant she was. Could stunts like this be why...?

"It feels great here on the roof."

Oblivious to my inner strife about her evaluation, Haneda stretched her hands into the air and looked up at the sky spread out above our heads. It was a beautiful and clear twilight sky. And like Haneda had pointed out, the wind was pleasant.

Haneda was a bull-headed shrike, a small orange bird around the size of a palm.

Maybe that's the reason.

When I looked at Haneda blending into the sunset, I thought:

She goes hand in hand with the sky.

She was standing a distance away with her head tilted up toward the heavens, but all of a sudden, she whirled around to face me. "So? Was this a good pick-me-up or what?"

"Oh, um! Y-yeah! I feel a little better, I think!"

I had been taken in by the sight of her. Snapped out of my reverie, I visibly fumbled my response.

Haneda's expression contorted. It looked like she was holding back laughter.

"Pfft, Mr. Hitoma… You're too funny."

"Sh-shut it… Anyway, Haneda, sorry, but intruding on the roof is a rule infraction, the consequence of which is a point deduction."

She had blatantly broken a rule in front of my eyes. As a teacher, I had no choice but to punish her.

"Okay. No problem. I'm gonna lose points anyway…"

She accepted the news readily and sauntered up to me.

As always, she came too close. But she didn't stop. She stepped closer and closer until we were nearly touching…!

This is giving me déjà vu!

She looked me up and down and grinned.

"Can you turn around for me, Mr. Hitoma?"

"What? Why?"

"Never mind. Just do it."

I didn't understand, but I turned my back toward her.

In the next moment, something soft pressed up against my back, and her arms came up under mine to circle around me.

C-could she be—?!

Huh?! No way. No way!
Is she hugging me from behind right now?!
No matter how you look at it, this is too forward, Haneda!! Aaah, girls sure are soft! No, stop! Don't be happy! Oh man, oh man, what is this pleasant feeling? I feel like I'm floating!
Huh—wait.

The sound of the wind changed.

We were ten meters in the air above the roof. By the time I had realized it, my feet were well off the ground.

"Ha-Ha-Ha-Ha-Ha-Haneda?!"

"Hmm?"

"W-w-w-w-we're floating—!"

"Of course. We're *actually* flying."

A large pair of orange wings spread from Haneda's back. I was soaring through the sky, supported in her arms.

"Ha-Ha-Haneda…!"

"What? Hold still, Mr. Hitoma, or else you're gonna fall."

"Fall…?!"

Don't be so flippant about something that horrific!

I had, in the past, been envious seeing depictions of flight made possible through magic, but flying in my imagination and in reality were two completely different things. Flying through the sky was actually really, really terrifying…!

The whooshing of the wind filled my ears. The breeze had been pleasant on the roof, but high up in the air, the sound stoked my fear.

"It's okay. Don't worry. If you just relax, I won't drop you," Haneda reassured me.

"No, look, this is terrifying! I'm legit freaking out here!!"

"Um, 'legit'? *Sigh…* Fine. You win…"

Again, my body seemed to come untethered. Haneda snaked her arms up beneath my knees and back, cradling me in her arms.

"Can you bring your arms around my neck, Mr. Hitoma?"

"Oh—yeah."

This was the first time I was being carried bridal-style by a girl.

But I felt immensely safer than I had a second ago. Haneda…was quite strong… I might have underestimated her, since she was a girl… This made me feel inferior in some way.

On top of that, a bridal carry was more…intimate…than I had expected…

The situation being what it was, my pulse sped up from nerves…

"You're not thinking anything weird, are you?" Haneda asked.

"No. Whatever could you mean?"

"Hmmmm. You've just been speaking all awkward and stiff for a while. Eh, it's amusing, so I'll let it slide."

I was too on edge to speak coherently; that was all.

She was having fun as always, teasing me… I could see her face now that we had changed positions.

And I could get a good look around me, too.

The sky was stained red, and the sun had set halfway.

"The sky from above is more infinite and beautiful than from the ground," Haneda said. "I wanted to show you this scenery."

Like Haneda said, the sky I saw as we flew through the air was expansive, ready to draw us into its embrace. The wind blowing in my ears wasn't as scary as it had been before.

The view was unparalleled.

This was what Haneda used to see.

"Mr. Hitoma." She peered out toward the setting sun. "I want to accept all of you, just like this sky."

"Wait. Are you asking me out—?"

"Don't get a complex."

"Sorry."

She rebuked me lightly, a little embarrassed, but I thought I finally understood why she had brought me here.

Haneda was the sky.

She may have many faces, but she was always there.

That was surely what she had brought me here to convey.

"…Thanks."

The word naturally slipped out.

Whispered in a voice so quiet, it may have gotten lost in the wind.

Haneda, lit golden by the setting sun, didn't reply, but a soft smile graced her mouth.

"Don't you think you've stacked up too many offenses in front of a teacher? You…might not be able to become human," I warned.

"Ah-ha-ha! That's fine. In fact, I'm happy you're evaluating me seriously."

"…Don't you want to become human?"

"Yeah. I do. But I don't have to just yet."

"What do you mean?"

"Hmm… That's a secret for now." Haneda smiled, but her expression looked just the tiniest bit sad.

The air in the sky was clear and pure. The sky spread out in all directions, unimpeded.

Perhaps there was more than one reason Haneda had brought me here.

In her avian form, she could see this view.

Was that the reason?

Was that why she had flagrantly broken the rules when I was watching?

In reality, she still wanted to be in the sky.

But what do I know?

I thought about saying something, but the descending curtain of twilight was so beautiful, it would be a waste to spoil it with words.

Haneda's hair gleamed in the light of the sun.

Beautiful.

They really do go hand in hand, the sky and her.

* * *

The sun set. A starry night sky spread out above the school roof.

The school was far from the city, so the air was clear. I could see more stars than back home.

Haneda and I returned to the roof; flying in the dark was too much of a risk.

It was a little chilly.

November—the season when it grew cold once the sun was gone. I asked Haneda if she was cold, and despite her thin clothing and the fact that she was still recovering, she replied, calm as you please, that this level of cold wasn't going to stop her.

Regardless of the reasons behind her actions, unhuman-like behavior was cause for deducting points. It grated on me to be playing exactly into her hands, supposing what she really wanted was to lose her points.

It was true that she had broken school rules and acted in an unhuman-like manner, but she had done it for the purpose of cheering me up.

As a teacher, outside of academic assessments, I could only subtract points from students. There was nothing else I could do in my position. Only other students could give out points.

If that was the case...

"Hey, Haneda," I said.

Back on solid ground, Haneda had tucked away her wings and was stretching lightly. She looked at me when I called her name.

"Hmm?"

"You like music, right?"

She grinned. "Yep, that's right. Both listening to it and singing."

I made my request. "Then can you let me hear you sing something? Right here, right now?"

"Here?!"

It was rash. But I wanted to hear it.

"In exchange for you watching the otoMAD video I made in the nurse's office. What do you think?"

"What? Taking you flying didn't count?"

"A blatant rule infraction like that? No, of course not."

"...Says the one who was enjoying himself."

"Well, I won't force you if you really don't want to."

Haneda averted her gaze and groaned. "Ugh, seriouslyyyy?" Then she peeked back at me and—

"...I'm not very good. Okay?"

She was being uncharacteristically timid and looked somewhat bash-ful. It was a novelty to see.

"Yeah, let's hear it."

I sat down near the door to the roof.

She directed a sullen look at me, but after a moment, she gave in and rolled her eyes, as if to say, *Ugh... Fine.*

Then she said, "...Just a little bit."

She straightened up and took a deep breath. A beat later, her soft, crystal voice rang out through the night sky.

She sang a song as resplendent as the glittering stars above.

What a lovely voice.

I hoped her gentle but powerful voice would travel far to the ears of many others.

To the ears of the students in the school.

To students who could reward her.

I was sure her starlit melody would not go unheard.

A **Misanthrope**
Teaches a Class for
Demi-Humans

Mr. Hitoma, Won't You Teach Us About Humans...?

The Misanthrope and the
Light of Dawn

A MISANTHROPE TEACHES A CLASS FOR DEMI-HUMANS

The previous year came and went. In swept January and the third semester. That day, as always, I was destined for a full day teaching in the classroom.

The classrooms were heated with kerosene stoves, but the hallways were so cold that it hurt. We might even see snow, according to the weather report. I glanced out the windows, internally praying for mercy, only to find the sky blanketed with a thick layer of clouds.

"Snow, huh…," I grumbled.

"You mean me?"

The sudden charming, bell-like voice made me jump.

"M-Ms. Saotome…?"

"Heh-heh! Your voice just cracked, Mr. Hitoma!"

The person I'd heard coming from behind me snickered over my reaction.

Ms. Saotome looked out the window expectantly. "I hope it snows today."

Ah, right. Her first name, Yuki, meant *snow* in Japanese.

I wonder if that makes her fond of snow…

"Do you like snow, Ms. Saotome?" I asked.

"I love it!"

Oof…!!

Her smile was so blinding, I thought I would melt and disappear beneath its light… In fact, of the two of us, Ms. Saotome was more suited to being the sun and I the snow.

I fell silent as I contemplated her smile.

"Um…Mr. Hitoma…?" She looked at me with concern. "Is something wrong?"

"Ah, um! Nope!" I answered hurriedly. "Hmm, let me see! Wh-what do you like about it?"

My follow-up question was distressingly banal. Huh? Socially awkward? Me?

Okay, fine, I admit it. But so what? I managed to survive these twenty-nine years, haven't I?

"What do I like about snow...? Hmmmm...," she mused. "There's so many things, it's hard to choose, but if I had to say, it's the fact that it's the reason why I ended up at this school!"

The reason she was here? My interest was piqued, but just then, the class bell rang.

It was time for me to part ways with Ms. Saotome temporarily... although I was reluctant to leave.

"See you, Mr. Hitoma. Let's talk another time." She waved and flitted away.

As I watched her go, I thought, *I hope one day I'll have the courage to call her Ms. Yuki.*

* * *

"What're you zoning out for? Stop staring out the window and start homeroom already!"

Usami's voice shook me from my idle thoughts about the weather and returned me to reality.

"Oh, my bad," I said.

Ah. I had an important announcement to share.

"Listen carefully, everyone. I have information about the advanced class's final assessment."

The mood instantly went from relaxed to tense.

The final assignment.

A significant factor in determining whether they would graduate.

The nature of the assessment was tailored to each individual student by the director and the principal.

I had asked about examples of previous assessments for reference. Some examples were:

Get ten thousand retweets on a text-only tweet.

Separate one kilogram of seven-chili-pepper seasoning into its seven base components.

Clear all stages of *Wreck*ng Crew*.

Anything goes, apparently.

"During first period tomorrow, you will meet with the principal in order of your roll-call numbers, at which time he will tell you about your particular assignment. You will have until the end of February to complete it. It may be difficult, but I hope you will all try your best to finish."

In other words, the final assignment was similar to a college graduation thesis paper. However, according to the principal, it was strictly an assignment, *not* a thesis. It was designed as a challenge to have the students master what couldn't be fully taught during classes.

While it did have a significant impact on their graduation prospects, it was also an important educational instrument, which was why even students for whom graduation was unlikely still had to turn it in.

The final assignment: insane and unpredictable.

What would this cohort be tasked with?

* * *

The next day, the advanced students met with the principal.

The sessions were conducted individually and in alphabetical order.

Once the preceding student returned, the next student would head to the principal's office.

Snug in the classroom, I watched over the students as they went one by one to the office, casually reading a light novel that had been released just the week prior.

I had given each of the students problem sets appropriate for their level to work on individually while they waited their turn.

Despite the cold snap the day before, it hadn't snowed. As I gazed out the window, I thought we were due the first snow of the season any day now.

The trees in the forest that had been so vibrant in the summer had shed their leaves. Some were completely bare.

It was a sunny and clear day. Oogami, who sat closest by the window, was filling out her worksheet somewhat drowsily.

The classroom door opened to reveal Minazuki, the last person on the list. She was back from the principal's office.

Evidently, everyone had already finished their work. Oogami was napping, Usami was doing problems for a different class that she had on hand, and Haneda was writing in her notebook.

Each of their meetings had taken around ten to fifteen minutes, and first period was nearly over. I dropped my gaze back to the book I was reading. I found that I could relate to these kinds of alternate-universe adventure stories more than before.

The bell rang to signal the end of the period.

I collected the worksheets from the students and quickly checked them over.

Minazuki broke the ice first. "Friends! What are your assignments?"

To me, Minazuki was a social butterfly who always helped take the lead at times like these to promote discussion in the class.

"The one asking should answer first," Usami said.

"Oh! I'm sorry, Usami. My assignment is a treasure hunt for one of the director's gems! Behold! These are hints on the gem's location!"

Minazuki took out a thin booklet and spread it open for everyone to see. Another oddball assignment. A treasure hunt sounded enjoyable.

"Ah, interesting," Usami mused. "Mine is to collect the signatures of every student and teacher in the school. They go in this notebook. They're underestimating me. It should be a piece of cake." She held out the notebook to Minazuki. "You first, Kyouka. I want you to sign here."

"Oh my! I'd be delighted!" Minazuki wrote her name, her pen skating across the page.

"You're the best. Thanks."

"'Kay, I'll go next," Haneda offered.

"Thanks, Tobari. What assignment did you get?"

"Me? Mm, compose the cheer for next year's sports festival."

"How wonderful! It suits you perfectly," Minazuki remarked.

"I guess. It's pretty much the same as the one I got last year. Hey, you awake, Isaki?"

Lulled by the warm sunlight, Oogami had fallen fast asleep at her desk, but she was sitting back up sleepily.

"*Yawn*... Sorry, everyone. I must've drifted off... Mm-ahhh..."

Her speech was fuzzy, as if her head had yet to clear.

"Good to have you back, Oogami. Can you turn in your worksheet?" I asked.

"Mm, yeah... Mr. Hitoma... Heeere..."

She tottered up to me with worryingly shaky steps. I took her worksheet and checked it over briefly.

Good. Looks like she filled in everything.

"By the way, what's your assignment?" I asked Oogami.

"Mngh... You're talking to me? Uhhh, write a novella with five or more characters and a minimum of ten thousand words."

"Wow!" Minazuki exclaimed. "You're an avid reader to be sure! It's a splendid task, perfect for you!"

"Do you think so...? *Ahem*, thanks, Kyouka."

"Isaki, write your name here." Usami handed Oogami the notebook after Haneda finished signing it.

"Oh, sure. Got it."

Since these were final assignments, I had assumed they would be harder to complete, but from what I had heard, they seemed surprisingly achievable. I was relieved.

Maybe that was how it was meant to be. These girls had grown over the last year, too.

I turned to leave the classroom, but Usami stopped me. "Hitoma, you're next. Don't go anywhere."

"Yeah, yeah."

The deadline is the end of February, but it seems like everyone's going to finish before the month is out.

I was reassured by the auspicious start.

I can't wait to see them reach the finish line.

* * *

One week passed after the final assignments were released.

Haneda had nearly completed her song.

She had submitted it to the principal for review several times and was in the middle of revising it according to his feedback.

Usami's project was coming along smoothly as well. In addition to the other advanced students, she had already collected signatures from all the teachers and intermediate students.

The problem was the beginner class.

Half of them still weren't used to their demi-human forms. Thus, they weren't great at writing.

It seemed that, originally, Usami had planned to collect thumb- and paw prints instead of names, but apparently they wouldn't count toward the assignment.

Signatures were signatures. Anything that wasn't the person's name written in their own hand was null and void.

To that end, after school, Usami was holding so-called "Usami's Cram Sessions" to teach the beginner students how to write their names properly.

Thanks to her efforts, nearly all the students could write their names now. She had only a little ways left to finish her assignment.

Oogami spent her days writing in silence.

Apparently, there were a few issues she had yet to figure out.

The biggest headaches were the five-plus characters. *Why would this character say something like this? Why can't they think the way I want them to? What is the relationship between these two?* Faced constantly with these kinds of questions, she was going to the language arts teacher every day for advice.

I don't understand other people's feelings..., she had complained. But then she had been struck with the realization, *If I don't, why don't I make an educated guess based on the character's position and the situation?* She didn't have all the answers, but she was giving it her all to press forward.

The problem was Minazuki.

The treasure hunt for the director's gem—she had been handed a sheaf of papers, the first page of which was a crossword puzzle.

The questions and answers all had to do with humans. A few had been tricky, but she'd managed to solve them.

However, her progress stopped at the second page.

Written on the page was, *Think back! Your first class! Follow the order. Pay them a visit to find...?*

And that was it.

First class? Did it mean the very first class she'd taken at this school? Or the first class as an advanced student? The clue was too abstract. She didn't understand. And what did "pay them a visit" mean?

For the time being, she was reenacting her first classes to the best of her memories.

February would mark the start of finals.

It was all too easy to get wrapped up in the final assignments, but needless to say, test scores also affected one's graduation prospects.

I had thought the assignments would be a breeze, but as the days went on, the atmosphere in the class grew steadily more frenzied.

* * *

"I'm done!"

Ten days had passed since the final projects were announced. The first to finish was Haneda.

She had managed to address all of the principal's feedback.

"Good work, Tobari! It's a fantastic song! I'm so happy for you that you finished," Minazuki said.

"Ah-ha-ha, thanks. What about you, Kyouka? How's your project going?"

"Ngh... I'm embarrassed to admit it, but I'm stumped..."

"Oh. Are you all right? Do you need help?"

"No, I couldn't possibly ask you for help! This assignment was given to me! I must complete it with my own abilities!"

"Okay. Well, let me know if you need anything. I'm here for you."

"I appreciate your concern." Minazuki smiled warmly.

Her expression discomfited me ever so slightly, but at the time, I had yet to understand the source of my unease.

Twelve days after the assignments were given, Oogami became the second person to finish.

She turned in her novella with five or more characters and a minimum of ten thousand words.

Her final word count was 38,033 words, more than triple the requirement.

Oogami had written a story set in a school.

She had let me read it. It was a slice-of-life story about the everyday life of a young girl with dual personalities. The writing style was rough around the edges, but in fact, it lent the work spice.

I only ever read light novels, and slice-of-life was hardly my favorite genre, but I liked the tale she had told.

I must admit, I could be a little biased because she's my student.

Upon completing her project, Oogami declared to me, "Storytelling isn't bad. I think I might like it."

Fifteen days in, Usami submitted her final assignment at long last.

Apparently, teaching the beginner students, especially the ones who weren't used to written language, had been a challenge.

She had accompanied them day after day, even when they ran from her or shrank away from her in fear or—unbelievably—laid traps for her… In conclusion, it had taken a toll on her.

Nonetheless, she had approached her underclassmen with persistence and patience and, with great pains, succeeded in having every single student write their names.

Usami had complimented her mentees, saying, "Those kids aren't unmotivated. It's just that they don't know how to apply themselves. I showed them which way to go, and they took off running. They did great." However, she tacked on a complaint under her breath. "But they're a bunch of naughty brats."

Nevertheless, her expression seemed happy to me.

The next day was the beginning of February.

The students would soon be busy studying for final exams.

As for Minazuki, she hadn't made any more progress on her assignment.

* * *

Sixteen days had passed. Classes were over for the day.

Her assignment at a standstill, Minazuki was feeling pressured.

"How is your project going, Kyouka…?" Oogami was the first to address the elephant in the room. "Um, uh, i-if perhaps there's anything I can do to help, I—I would be happy to, so please don't hesitate to ask."

"Thank you!" Minazuki said. "But you're busy studying for finals, right? I'll keep trying to the best of my ability for a while longer!" Her lips curved into an elegant smile.

It was a gentle refusal.

For a moment, Oogami looked unsure, but then she pressed her lips together and forged ahead.

"Are you positive, Kyouka? I was taught that I have to convey what I'm thinking using my words, otherwise the other person won't understand, so here goes. Um, I hope I'm not being too pushy, but…if you need help, please tell me. I mean it!"

Minazuki wavered at the normally meek Oogami's rare show of persistence.

However, soon, she smiled faintly and said in her usual tone, "I will. I'll let you know."

Haneda and Usami observed in silence.

* * *

Day seventeen. Morning.

I had just finished listing the day's announcements.

"Kyouka." Usami, her expression dark, turned to Minazuki. "Tell me what you're stuck on in your assignment. I'll help."

"Thank you for the offer, Usami! But it's all right! This is my problem to solve!" Minazuki was clearly worn out, but she worked to put on a bright face.

Displeased, Usami clicked her tongue. "Do you really believe that?"

"What?"

"Your smile has always rubbed me the wrong way," Usami said. "It reminds me of someone else who used to force themselves to smile, someone I love. It feels like you're pretending."

"I'm not. I face my problems with a smile, and I'm proud of myself for it… It's true that I might be pushing myself, but…that's what I want. It's an obstacle I want to challenge and overcome, so I am all right."

"…Rrrgh! I can't stand that attitude of yours!"

Silence fell over the classroom.

Usami's expression was angry, but it also looked like she was on the verge of tears.

"U-Usami…," I stammered, unsure what to do.

"It's okay, Mr. Hitoma," Minazuki said.

"Minazuki…"

I had intended to try to get them to reconcile, but Minazuki impeded my attempt.

"Usami, the final assignments are meaningful because we are meant to tackle them alone, don't you think? I won't borrow anyone else's power in order to complete my task. I am grateful you are worried about me, but your concern is unnecessary. Please, can I ask for your understanding?" Minazuki said, exceedingly polite.

Still looking like she was about to cry, Usami urged Minazuki, "You're taking on too much by yourself. Will you…really ask for help when you need it?"

"I—" Minazuki's words caught in her throat, but she immediately composed herself. "I do not need help."

A lofty, arrogant proclamation.

Usami visibly reined herself in, perhaps knowing Minazuki wouldn't listen even if she was to argue further, and returned to her seat without another word.

Haneda and I could do nothing but watch their argument quietly. Oogami's tail was sweeping from side to side agitatedly.

Final exams start next week. Is everything going to be okay…?

* * *

Another two weeks came and went. It had been a month since the final projects were assigned. Finals were already over.

As far as the exams went, according to the score reports, all the advanced students had received good marks.

But Minazuki had yet to finish her assignment. She and Usami didn't see eye to eye on that front, and ever since their disagreement, it seemed to me that their relationship had only grown more strained.

They hadn't argued again, but they barely spoke to each other. The class's atmosphere was icy…

Ugh—I don't want to go to class…

I dragged myself toward the classroom for morning homeroom; my legs felt like they were made of lead.

Should I do something...? No, if I say something careless... Aw, man, what do I do...? Should I leave it alone? I have no clue what the best solution is...

The gorgeous weather was at complete odds with my feelings. For some reason, I felt as if the heavens were shaking their finger at me.

"Oh, Mr. Hitomaaaa! Good morning!"

I found myself hugged from behind all of a sudden, and I let out an unwitting yelp.

"Uwah!! Uh... O-Oogami..."

Ohhh... Today's the full moon.

Oogami twirled around to stand in front of me.

It was quite cold, but Full-Moon Oogami's outfit showed a lot of skin as usual. I found myself soothed by this bubbly Oogami. She was like a ray of sun cutting through the clouds.

"Hey! What's the beef between Kyouka and Ushami?!" she demanded.

"Oh... About that... How do I put it...?" I mumbled.

"Kyouka's assignment is a mess, and Ushami butted in out of worry, right?"

"You already know everything!"

"I mean, I do share almost all the other Isaki's memories, you know? What do you make of this sitch, Mr. Hitoma?"

"Don't link arms with me like we're buds."

Oogami had a liberal sense of personal space by nature, and the closeness sent my thoughts flying in undesirable directions.

"Boo. Stingy." She puffed out her cheeks in displeasure and moved away from me. "Well? What do you think?"

"Uh, I'm not in any posi—"

"Give it a rest. I'm trying to have a serious talk here."

Her sudden no-nonsense attitude blindsided me.

I opened my mouth reluctantly. "...I think it's important to recognize the things we *can't* do with our own power."

"Makes sense, maybe?"

"It's surprisingly important to be able to rely on those around us."

"All right, okay..."

Oogami laid a hand on her chin. She looked like she was thinking. Then a light bulb seemed to go off in her head, and she snapped back to face me:

"I know! Have you ever had an octobash, Mr. Hitoma?"
"...A what now?"

* * *

Rei Hitoma. Human. Twenty-nine years old. In the advanced classroom of Shiranui High, I attended my first-ever *takoyaki* party, aka octobash, where we made the popular grilled dough balls stuffed with octopus.

But it wasn't an actual octopus.

Why? Because we hadn't been able to get our hands on one. As a substitute, we were using *konnyaku*, a firm gelatin made of devil's tongue plant. So, to be accurate, we were holding a *konnyaku* party, aka a devil bash...? That sounded really suspicious...

"There's no harm to our ocean friends, since we're using *konnyaku*, so I can eat with a clear conscience!!" Minazuki said.

"Which camp are you in when it comes to seaweed, Kyouka? Sprinkle it on or leave it off?" Oogami asked.

"On! Seaweed used to be my staple food!"

"I want to try grilling the batter, Mr. Hitoma," Oogami said.

Usami chimed in. "Me too."

"Okay, okay. Next round's all yours," I said.

The *konnyaku* party was a strategy devised by Oogami and yours truly.

According to Oogami, even the most serious concerns were easily aired while cooking and eating a meal together. That was the gist.

Besides that, she had seen some model or idol post about their own octobash on social media, and she had been envious.

Despite there being no octopus or bonito fish flakes in our pseudo-*takoyaki*, the students seemed to enjoy Oogami's party anyway.

"So spill. How's your assignment, Kyouka?"

Oogami's blunt question caused the room to freeze momentarily.

"…I'm working through it the best I know how!"

"Wow, great!!" Oogami said. "What do you have to do? I'm fuzzy on everyone's projects. I want to know!!"

That was a lie.

Oogami Tactic Number 1: pretend to know nothing, grill Minazuki about the details, and confirm her current status.

"I was given a treasure hunt!" Minazuki answered.

"Oh my god! Treasure! Sounds fun! But, like…how are you supposed to find it?"

"By solving puzzles! The principal gave me a booklet of them. The answers will lead me to the treasure!"

"Oh, don't tell me there's more than one problem? That sucks! That must be super difficult! It sounds like too much!"

"You're right… The first puzzle was a challenge, but I managed to figure it out! It was a crossword, and the clue was 'Gotemba.'"

You call that a clue? It sounds like its own puzzle.

"Ah! I've heard of it!! The outlet mall! Everyone's buzzing about it!!"

"Oh? Is it really?"

"Yeah, really! There's a hot spring, too! On my feed, there was a model talking about how close it is to Mount Fuji!"

"You know everything, Isaki…!" Minazuki was restless now that a golden nugget about her project had unexpectedly fallen into her lap.

"By the way, you said that was the first puzzle, right? What's the second one like?"

"It's—" Minazuki's face clouded over like she found it hard to continue.

Her expression spoke volumes. Oogami and I could guess what the situation was.

The conclusion was obvious. She was still stuck on the second problem. She must not have made any progress since the last time I had asked.

Tactic Number 1, confirm the current status: complete.

On to Tactic Number 2: ask about the details and lend a hand wherever it seemed possible.

"Let me guess. The second puzzle must be a monster! Like a killer math problem!" Oogami buried her face in her hands and moaned, "I suck at math!"

Her strength was undeniably in the humanities. Her math grades were, admittedly, not great.

Haneda and Usami were absorbed in making more octopus-less *takoyaki*—or pretending to be. They paid no attention to the batter starting to burn in the *takoyaki* grill pan in front of them.

"The second puzzle...is a riddle of sorts...," Minazuki finally said.

Oogami tilted her head and played dumb. She gave Minazuki a blank stare and asked, "You have to solve a riddle?"

"Yes. 'Think back! Your first class! Follow the order. Pay them a visit to find...?' That's what it says. I tried looking at it from all sorts of perspectives—my first class as a beginner student and then intermediate and advanced, too—but I still don't understand..."

"What *was* our first beginner class? I don't remember at all!"

"It was an overview about the school," Usami said. "After that, we were given a handout about *hiragana*, and then we learned to introduce ourselves. The beginner students start with speaking and writing. We didn't get our first textbooks until we became intermediate students."

"That's exactly right," Minazuki agreed.

This was the first time she and Usami had spoken in a while.

"Kyouka... Do you remember what we had to say when we first introduced ourselves?" Usami asked awkwardly but gently.

"What did we say...?"

"Our names and our reason for becoming human."

"Simple is king!" Oogami cut in. "Oooh, me first! 'Isaki Oogami! I want to become human to graduate from this half-baked existence and live as one single person.' That's what I think I said, but that's been put on hold! I'm in the middle of rethinking my entire life! Highly recommend it! But for safety reasons, I still want to be human!"

"Oh, are we reintroducing ourselves now? Sounds like fun," Haneda said. "My name is Tobari Haneda. My reason is because I want to play music."

"What's with this development? Fine, I'll play along. Sui Usami. I want to repay a human who took care of me, and that's why I want to help the people around me. So—Kyouka, I'm sorry for before."

Minazuki jumped at being addressed out of the blue. "Pardon…?"

"I wasn't thinking about your dedication to trying your best. I wanted to help, but it was self-centered."

"Usami… No, you don't have to… It's not your fault." Minazuki's troubled eyes roved. Usami watched her with worry. "I'm sorry. I was the one who…um…"

Seeing that she was at a loss for what to say, I spoke up. "Minazuki."

Minazuki had a strong sense of responsibility.

Maybe that was the part of her who was descended from Poseidon.

I couldn't imagine the pressure and strife she had faced in her position. Relying carelessly on the wrong person could have been a fatal mistake.

But here…here, she was Kyouka Minazuki. An average student.

So—

"This is merely my opinion. I don't know what it's like for you, but I…I can't accomplish anything without help from others," I said.

—*I'll tell her about me. About the foolish and hopeless me.*

"I'm not…great at stringing sentences together, so whenever I have to write up the announcements, I always ask Mr. Hoshino to look it over. There's tons of aspects about classes I'm not used to, either, so I'm constantly going to Ms. Saotome for help—"

Since I'd come to this school, those two had saved me more times than I could count.

"What I want to say is, you know, maybe that's just what humans are like. There are plenty of things I've been asked to do, but I can't by myself. That's when it's important to ask someone for help. You might not think so, but to me, that's a crucial skill."

To live by oneself—what a reckless idea.

We lean on others, are leaned on by others. By holding each other up in this way, we live on.

Minazuki's pride was pure and beautiful, I thought, but it was fragile at the same time.

"…May I?"

The words were whispered so softly, they seemed to fade and disappear.

"May I borrow a few moments of everyone's valuable time?"

"I already said it's fine," Usami replied.

"I'm on board, too," Haneda agreed.

"You betcha! Of course!" Oogami exclaimed. "I might be good at riddles. You never know!"

Minazuki grew teary at the others' replies. Her expression softened like ice thawing. "You guys…!"

"Oh, I'm here, too, if you need me," I added belatedly.

"Yes, please, Mr. Hitoma…!"

Then Minazuki went to her desk and took out a thin booklet. "I apologize for imposing on you during this busy season, but…please lend me a hand!"

* * *

With our bellies pleasantly full, we brought our party to an end and switched to a riddle-solving session as a class.

The first to spot something was Usami.

"…Could 'first class' be a hint to use the school guide and the *hiragana* handout to solve the puzzle?"

"What do you mean?" Minazuki asked.

"I've been teaching the beginner students the alphabet the whole time, so I still have the *hiragana* chart. Give me a second." Usami fumbled through her bag and found the handout. "Look. This is what we got during our first class. What if we lay it on top of the school map and see where the *hiragana* of the first clue you got overlap? 'Gotemba,' was it? So four *hiragana* characters. Then we can trace out a path—or something. What do you think? That could be the order to follow."

"Really? Isn't that too contrived?" Haneda said.

"Oh, but here! Don't the map and chart stack perfectly?! That's obviously the answer!!" Oogami exclaimed.

Isn't that because they're both printed on A3 paper…? Well, it is a little contrived, but there's no harm in trying it out.

"Let's go!" Minazuki said. "What's first…? The ground-floor culinary arts prep room, then the ground-floor staff room, the beginner classroom… No, the hedges in front of it… Is that right…? And finally, the library!"

All the members of the advanced class set off for the places on the chart.

As a result:

"It's here!"

Taped on the back of every door was a small envelope with *Kyouka Minazuki: Final Assignment* written on it. The assignments had been announced long ago. The fact that the envelopes had gone undiscovered the entire time must mean these locations were not frequented by students.

In the envelopes were the following notes: *A certain love story, A place in a dream, Teacher, Advanced-class student.*

Their meaning was a complete mystery.

"Is this referring to which of us you have feelings for, Mr. Hitoma?" Minazuki guessed.

"Uh, no, absolutely not."

Obviously, I was obligated to shoot down the suggestion.

"Hmmmm, are you suuure?" Oogami teased.

"Oogami… You shouldn't mess with people…"

This brat… Stop jumping up and picking on me every time the subject of romance comes up…

"What does it say in your booklet?" Usami asked.

"It says, 'Where does the confession take place?'"

"…Huh? I don't get it. What about you, Isaki?"

"Wha—? Ngh?! M-me?!" she yelped. "Wh-wh-wh-why me…? Aaaaah, um…uh…Mr. Hitomaaa…"

"What?!"

The way she was staring at me with tears in her eyes, it made it seem as if something unthinkable had happened between us.

Wh-what happened to the vibe?!

"Mr. Hitoma, you couldn't have…!" Haneda said.

"Whatever it is you're imagining, you're wrong! Probably wrong! Come on, Oogami! Say something!"

"But I…shouldn't…," she mumbled.

"Why?!"

"…! It's not about me but the other Isaki, so I can't just blurt it out!"

"Hitoma, did something actually happen between you two?!" Usami demanded.

"I seriously have no idea what she's talking about!" I protested.

"That's right! Ushami! Between the other me and Mr. Hitoma? Not in a million years!"

Agh…! I'm glad she told the truth, but it hurts to hear it said so bluntly…!

"Then what are you referring to?" Minazuki, the assignee of the riddle in question, asked.

"Kyouka…! Aaaah…! Um…" Oogami was having difficulty speaking. She bit her lip. "Ummm…well, the other Isaki's final assignment…"

Oh.

That was enough to help me figure out the next location.

Minazuki and the others had yet to solve the puzzle. No surprise there; the hint was referring to the novella Oogami had written for her project, to one particular scene in the youth drama.

Which raised the question, why had the school given Minazuki this puzzle? Was the person responsible able to see the future?

"Ngh…! Sorry! I can't say anything more than this! The other me will be back tomorrow, so ask her! Sorry, Kyouka!" Oogami bowed in apology to Minazuki.

"Not at all! It's not a big deal! I'm the one asking you for assistance! Quite the opposite—I'm thankful for your hint! I'll ask Isaki again tomorrow."

Thanks to the help of the other advanced students, Minazuki was making leaps and bounds on her final assignment.

* * *

The next day, with Isaki Oogami as our guide, we ended up near the barrier at the cherry blossom tree.

Stepping past the tree would take us into the outside world.

The first time I set foot on these premises, the cherry blossoms had been in full bloom, unforgettable in their splendor. At the moment, tightly closed buds were sprouting from the tips of a few branches. The blossoms were in the middle of their preparations to usher in a new spring.

"It should be around here…," Oogami mumbled.

In her story, there was a student who was in love with a teacher. One day, that student dreamed she confessed to him.

The setting was before a large cherry blossom tree.

"Um, my story took place underneath a cherry blossom tree. I don't think I'm mistaken… Agh, maybe I got ahead of myself…"

"Don't be so wishy-washy! Let's just try and search first!" Usami said.

"That's right! If we can't figure it out, we can put our heads together again," Haneda added.

The students scoured the area under the tree. I watched over them from a distance.

Among the scattered buds, I thought I could see something glittering.

At first, I dismissed it as the sunlight reflecting off the morning mist, but it wasn't.

It was a box.

High in the branches was a small, ornate box.

I had seen those embellishments before. It'd been during summer vacation—

"Minazuki, look…!"

I pointed the box out to Minazuki, who was rummaging around the tree.

"Oh my…!" she cried.

We were probably at the end of the hunt. Inside the box was surely one of the director's jeweled rings.

Oogami looked up at the box and mumbled, "Wow, it's quite high…"

It was so high, there was no way you could reach it with your hand. Most likely, you wouldn't be able to take it down without climbing the tree.

"If we shake the tree, do you think it will fall down?" Minazuki asked me.

"Hmm…I don't know. It looks pretty secure."

"Well, I'll give it a try! Here I go!"

Minazuki tackled the tree, but it didn't so much as quiver.

To me, it totally looked like she was hugging the tree. A heartwarming sight.

"…You suck," Usami said exasperatedly.

Unfortunately, I agreed.

"Oh, what if we throw something at it?" Haneda suggested. "You know, as if we were playing darts or doing target practice."

"Ah! Tobari! What a wonderful idea! Hmm… Let's see…" Minazuki spun around, but she couldn't find a single stone or stick to throw.

The area around the cherry blossom tree was unnaturally clear, like it had been tidied.

Minazuki was staring fixedly at the tree branches as if she was debating breaking one off herself, but then she shook her head.

Haneda approached her holding a feather.

"Oh, ah, Tobari… Thank you so much! It is horribly uncouth for me to impose on you, but may I please use one of your feathers to bring down the box…?" Minazuki asked.

"Hmm? Heh-heh, nope!" Haneda smirked.

Minazuki wilted. "B-but…!"

Haneda squatted down in order to catch Minazuki's eyes. "It's a 'no' if you ask with that guilty look on your face. Lighten up, and I'll give you however many you want."

Minazuki looked at Haneda with a strange expression. "You want me to 'lighten up'…?"

"Yep. Being polite is nice and all, but you sounded so stuffy, it gave me a scare."

…I doubted she had felt any such thing.

But I understood what she was trying to say.

Minazuki muttered, "Stuffy…?" and mulled it over.

Then, having decided what she wanted to say, she turned back toward Haneda.

"Tobari! Help me out! I would like one feather, please!"

"Okay! Here you go."

My guess was that she hadn't liked the way Minazuki had put herself down when asking the first time.

Being self-deprecating and showing courtesy to others were two completely different things.

Minazuki took the orange feather from Haneda.

Then she took aim at the box and threw the feather straight at it.

On her first throw, the box twitched, but it didn't fall.

On her second throw, she hit the box dead center, and it wobbled violently.

However, it still didn't fall. Compared to before, it was now in a much more precarious position.

Her third throw missed the mark.

But at that very moment, a strong gust of wind blew, shaking the tree.

The box lifted from the branches, hovering in the air.

"It's going to fall…!" Minazuki cried.

A cheer erupted from the students. Minazuki went running in the direction the box flew in order to catch it. She wasn't a fast runner, but it was a short distance. She should make it. The end of her assignment was in sight.

Huh? Wait, isn't that the direction of the bus stop?

Which means…the box is flying outside the barrier!

"No! Minazuki! Stoppppp!!!!" I screamed at Minazuki's back.

Startled by my loud shout, she turned around toward me. She stopped just short of the barrier. If she had gone two more steps, we would've been in hot water. She was in the clear.

But the box was slowly falling toward the ground.

If it smashed into the ground, it could break! And then Minazuki's assignment would be—

I was the only one who could catch it outside the barrier.

Damn it! When was the last time I had to sprint like this?!

I took off running at full speed.

My muscles are gonna be in pain tomorrow!

The box dropped lower.

Just a little more. Just a little more—!

Am I gonna make it?! Forget that. I'll make sure I do!!

The box was inches from smashing into the ground. I reached out my hand desperately—

"Ha-ha… Safe."

I tumbled gracelessly to the forest floor, but held firmly in my grip was the small, ornamental box.

My budget suit that I had bought for 30,000 yen and had worn only twice was covered in dirt, but that was a cheap price to pay for the box's safety.

That was my first-ever sliding catch.

"Are you injured, Mr. Hitoma…?!" Minazuki shouted from inside the barrier. She must have been worried when I yelled out and took off running all of a sudden… But I was glad she was okay.

"Yeah, I'm fine!" I replied. "And the box is, too!"

"…! Thank goodness…!" She collapsed limply to the ground.

The other three were beside Minazuki. They huddled around her and looked to be saying something, but I couldn't hear anything from where I was.

I tightened my grip around the small box and got up to reenter the barrier.

They all worked hard.

With that, the final assignments of the advanced students were all complete.

I started walking back toward the barrier.

At that moment, I caught a glimpse of a stout shadow coming up behind the students.

Before I could say anything, the person burst out in front of the class.

"My dear advanced students! A big, big, *big* congratulations to you!!!!" The principal's jolly voice boomed through the quiet forest.

...Outdoors—or, to be more precise, surrounded by nature—he looked even more out of place than usual.

The reason he looked at home in the principal's office was probably because the office defied the norm, too.

"Let's have a look-see. Minazuki's final assignment is... Hmm? Where is it?"

He circled Minazuki with mincing steps, twisting his head to look all around him.

From an outsider's perspective, he would look like a little old man following a beautiful girl...

In fact...he was one wrong step away from being mistaken for a suspicious individual... Seriously...

"Ah, Principal Karasuma, my assignment is over there," Minazuki said, gesturing to me. "It crossed the barrier, so Mr. Hitoma went to retrieve it for me—"

The principal turned in the direction she was pointing, and his eyes fell on me. "Mr. Hitoma! You're covered in dirt! What a predicament! I'll lend you the backup suit I keep in my office just in case, and you can wear it home!"

...*That is a fate I want to avoid at all costs*, I thought as I returned to the barrier, taking my time, since I had exhausted my energy in my desperate dash.

* * *

I handed the box to Minazuki when I was back across the barrier.

"Here you are."

"Thank you very much...!" She carefully opened it to check the contents.

In the middle of the box sat a ring identical to mine, a ring with one of the director's gems embedded into it. Having verified that the contents were what was expected, Minazuki shut the box and walked over to the principal.

"I'm sorry to keep you waiting, Principal. I wasn't able to finish my assignment by myself. However, with the assistance of my wonderful friends, I managed to complete it. Therefore, I would like to request that my points be split equally among us four, please." She bowed deeply to him.

He smiled without saying anything.

"Here is the treasure I was asked to find." Minazuki held out the box to the principal.

The finely decorated box was as beautiful as always. He took it from her, ran a hand over it like it was something precious, and slipped it into his pocket.

"Once again, congratulations, Minazuki."

The principal spun to look at each of the advanced students in turn: Tobari Haneda, Isaki Oogami, Sui Usami, and finally Kyouka Minazuki.

"All of the assignments have been submitted," he said in a kind but solemn voice. "With that, the students who have met the requirements for graduation have been decided."

I was caught off guard by the sudden announcement, but I found myself waiting with anticipation.

The students who had met the requirements for graduation...

The atmosphere was tense.

Graduation—the goal of every student here.

"The total number of students graduating this year is one. This student has no infractions and has accrued points at a steady pace. Her academic ability and adaptability toward human society leaves nothing to be desired. Her one weak point was asking others for help. This student has always tried to solve her problems herself. However, in the course of this final assignment, she was able to rely on those around her and has learned to properly 'make a nuisance' of herself..."

Someone gulped.
The principal opened his mouth slowly.

"The student with the aforementioned traits eligible for graduation is you, Kyouka Minazuki."

A **Misanthrope**
Teaches a Class for
Demi-Humans

Mr. Hitoma, Won't You Teach Us About Humans...?

The Misanthrope and the Long-Awaited Graduation Ceremony

A MISANTHROPE TEACHES A CLASS FOR DEMI-HUMANS

I stared out the window of the bus, rocked by the swaying motion. The scenery was the familiar one I saw every day: a narrow, single-laned road winding up the mountain with nothing else around. The bus spat me out at my stop as usual and continued to its next destination.

It was already March, but the wind remained chilly. Still, it carried the faint scent of grass. Spring was here. Leaves were sprouting on a few of the trees in the forest.

Before I had come to this school, I had never paid attention to the trees and their changes throughout the seasons.

After I got off the bus, I took the lane next to the bus stop to the school like always.

The buds on the cherry blossom tree standing just within the barrier had yet to bloom.

It was the day of the graduation ceremony.
Kyouka Minazuki's graduation ceremony.

* * *

I wasn't used to such ceremonies.

The formality made me break out in hives.

The entire student body attended.

Since we were in the middle of the forest, the gymnasium was cold, and gas heaters had been placed around the room to warm the space. To be precise, we teachers had moved them here just for the ceremony.

Once it started, the students would have to line up in their designated places, but in the meantime, they were free to crowd around the stoves and soak in as much warmth as they liked.

I was just wondering if they would accept me into their herd when Ms. Saotome approached me.

"The ceremony will start soon, Mr. Hitoma. Let's line up the students," she said.

"Oh, yes. I'll get right on that."

For the occasion, Ms. Saotome had tied her hair not in a low ponytail like she usually did but in a high bun... The contrast between the polished look and her bubbly personality was irresistible.

I went over to the advanced students and had them line up. The class was positioned on the far left side from the entrance.

Minazuki was no longer in the group.

Instead, this entire time, she had been standing next to the principal.

The beginner and intermediate classes were lining up, too. Some of the beginner students couldn't stand the cold and refused to leave the heater, so Mr. Hoshino had brought in one of the standby heaters.

And so the graduation ceremony began.

* * *

After a long speech from the principal came the director's remarks, which were read by the facilitator, Ms. Saotome. Everything was right on track.

In the end, an entire year had passed without my meeting the director once.

They weren't even able to attend the graduation ceremony—just how busy must they be?

The director of the school... Could they be a prominent figure in the country? It was terrifyingly plausible. Or maybe they didn't actually exist at all... Hmm, what could the truth be...?

"We will now confer the degree." Ms. Saotome's clear voice resounded throughout the gym. "Kyouka Minazuki."

"Present!" Minazuki said loudly and slowly walked toward the podium with careful steps.

She must've been nervous. The stairs surely felt like they led up to the stage of her dreams.

Minazuki was cheerful, positive, and had an unshakable sense of self.

And she had learned the art of relying on others when the going got tough.

Minazuki faced the principal across the podium.

"Ms. Kyouka Minazuki. Congratulations," he said.

"Thank you for taking care of me these three years," she replied.

He handed her the diploma.

When the new school year began, she would no longer be part of the advanced class.

She would leave the school and begin her life in the world of humans.

She was already standing firmly on her two legs.

*　*　*

After the graduation ceremony, I went to the advanced classroom. Minazuki wasn't there.

"*Sigh*. It's finally over. Good job, everyone," I told the class. "Minazuki has various paperwork she needs to complete, but I've been told she'll come back here in a little while."

After it had been confirmed that she would graduate, she'd been running around nonstop.

She had a mountain of things to prepare for her life after the advanced class. Starting this spring, she would be enrolling in a dance school, apparently.

She should have no problems with her day-to-day life, since that was a prerequisite to graduate, but she still had her hands full with securing housing, furniture, and other daily necessities.

Currently, she was finalizing the details with the principal and going through anything else that needed to be discussed.

* * *

"Let's see. The new semester starts April eighth. The details are on the printout I passed around, so make sure you read it. If there's anything you don't understand, ask me or one of the other teachers. Any questions?" I asked.

"Yeah," Usami said. "Are there any new students joining the advanced class?"

"Ah, I'm curious about that, too, but I haven't heard anything yet. That's something to look forward to for next year. Anyone else?"

…No one replied. Oogami was skimming the handout, and Haneda looked bored like always.

"All right, then that's all from me. See you next year," I said.

At that moment, the door opened. The leading lady of the day stepped into the room with a bundle of papers in her arms.

"I'm sorry to interrupt. I'm back!" Minazuki said.

"You're not interrupting. We just finished," I said.

Everything around her was going to change. No doubt her to-do list was even longer than what I was imagining.

"Welcome back, Kyouka…!" Oogami said.

"You took forever. Did something gnarly hold you up?" Haneda asked.

"Kyouka! I have so much to ask you!" Usami added.

The last time we had seen Minazuki was when she had been standing up onstage. The moment she stepped inside the classroom, she was surrounded by the advanced students.

"When are you going to become human?" Usami asked Minazuki.

"The day after tomorrow."

"Where are you going to live after this?" Oogami asked. "Did you rent an apartment?"

"I'll be living near my new school. I'll make ends meet with the scholarship money I received from the director."

"You're going to a dance school, right? Do you think it'll be tough?" Haneda said.

"The curriculum is pretty packed. But I'll do my best to succeed!"

Minazuki answered the barrage of questions with no hesitation. Her expressions were animated and rich, like any other high school girl.

"I'm not saying I'll be lonely," Usami said, "but this year wasn't horrible."

"It's okay, Usami—I know you'll miss Kyouka. She's the life and soul of the party," Haneda commented.

"Kyouka! This is a letter from the other me—from Isaki!"

"You guys… Thank you…! Thanks to all your support, I know I can keep moving forward."

Minazuki looked happy surrounded by the classmates who she'd been studying alongside this entire year.

"Minazuki," I said.

"Mr. Hitoma!" She turned to me and smiled softly. "Thank you for your help this year."

"That's my line. The road ahead won't be easy, but if you ever find yourself in a pinch, you can always contact us here at the school."

"I'm grateful." She bowed to me. "Mr. Hitoma. When I was working on my final assignment, you told me about your own failings, and for that, I would like to thank you. I…wanted to be perfect. That was what I aimed for my entire life. But I was wrong. Humans are imperfect. I myself am imperfect… The reason I can stand tall is because I have help from others."

At the end, she whispered under her breath, "That was surely what my assignment was meant to tell me."

"Mr. Hitoma! Thank you for teaching me how to be human!"

"Thank you, too, for letting me be your teacher."

The words emerged from my mouth so naturally, even I was surprised.

Because of these students, I was able to become a teacher once more. Minazuki smiled warmly again and rejoined the others.

"Nooo, Kyouka! Please don't forget about us!" Oogami cried.

"Isaki… Don't worry. I won't."

Usami spotted a small box buried among Minazuki's pile of documents and asked, "That box… Is it the same one from your assignment?"

"Yes, that's right. This is one of the director's jeweled rings, the same one teachers wear." Minazuki cradled the box in both hands. "Once we become human, our memories of the school and before we enrolled get replaced, remember? But by putting on this ring, all the memories will come back. It's a congratulations present just for new graduates, apparently! Plus, as long as I have it, I can reenter the school barrier, too!"

Ahhh, so basically the same conditions I got.

"Kyouka! Guys! How about we throw a girls' night at the dorms today to celebrate…?! I still want to keep talking with you!"

It was rare for Oogami to suggest a plan herself. She, too, was changing.

"How wonderful! I would love to!" Minazuki said.

"If you insist," Usami added. "I suppose I'll join you."

"Y'know, staying in touch is going to be tough once she leaves. How about you try being honest for once?"

"…No one asked you, Tobari."

"Heh-heh. I see right through you, Usami. I know you're just lashing out to hide your embarrassment!" Minazuki teased.

"Ugh! No one asked *you*, either!"

"It looks like we're all in agreement. Then it's decided. We'll hold girls' night in my room today!" Oogami exclaimed. "Oh, Mr. Hitoma… Will you join us as well?"

"But then it wouldn't be a girls' night, right? Besides…I can't enter the dorms anyway."

I could practically see the question marks floating above Oogami's head, but she appeared to accept my answer. All she said in reply was, "Okay, I understand. That's too bad."

The day after tomorrow, Minazuki was going to leave this school and begin her life as a human.

Seeing the class fired up over their party plans, I thought that it would be nice if this time Minazuki spent with her friends would become memories she would never forget.

* * *

It was the night of the graduation ceremony.

Once a year, the teachers held a feast in one of the conference rooms. Granted, it was a pretty casual affair. The party was BYOB, and Roost Rep Ryouko prepared finger foods for the staff to peck at. Simple and sweet.

How long has it been since I last drank with coworkers?

I had rarely been invited out at my previous workplace, so it was possible the last time was during my part-time job in college. I wasn't a heavy drinker, but I could manage a few drinks to keep others company.

"Your glass is empty, Mr. Hitoma. Do you want a refill?"

"Oh, Ms. Saotome...! Thank you!"

I'd planned to stop at one drink, but if Ms. Saotome was the one insisting, how could I refuse? I decided to take her up on her offer.

A slow stream of beer waterfalled from the bottle Ms. Saotome had brought over into my cup. I said my thanks and took a sip.

Mmmmm, this beer Ms. Saotome poured just for me is crazy good.

"Can you hold your liquor, Mr. Hitoma?" Mr. Hoshino asked. His cheeks were a little flushed. Maybe he was a lightweight.

I answered honestly. "Um, to a degree, but I wouldn't say I'm a strong drinker."

"Oh dear! I'm sorry," Ms. Saotome said. "I didn't mean to pressure you. Tell me if you can't drink any more!"

"You're the one who drinks like a fish, Ms. Yuki," Mr. Hoshino said, exasperated.

"Hey! Don't be mean, Mr. Hoshino! I just like sake!! That's all!"

Wow, so Ms. Saotome is a sake fan. Maybe I should study up on it.

The alcohol was making it hard to think. Though that could be the spark needed to bring us closer together.

"I don't believe it for a second. How many drinks have you had again?" Mr. Hoshino asked.

Ms. Saotome averted her eyes and pointed hesitantly at the four empty twenty-four-ounce bottles.

Four.

Four!

"…Um, errr."

Ms. Saotome peeked at Mr. Hoshino guiltily like a kid caught red-handed while playing a prank.

He didn't respond, but he looked angry. "…Didn't I tell you to cut back on drinking outside the house?"

"*Ack!* I'm so sorry! But…but! We only get to celebrate like this once a year! It's only natural to drink when I'm in such a festive mood!"

"Stop trying to defend yourself!"

That's unexpected… Ms. Saotome is…a heavy drinker…

Noticing my peculiar stare, Ms. Saotome scrambled to explain. "Eep! Mr. Hitoma, it's all a misunderstanding! Actually, I'm an ex–*yuki onna*. A snow-woman spirit! I'm just good at drinking because I used to live in a cold region! I'm not the kind of lowlife who drowns themself in drink…! I'm begging you, Mr. Hitoma! Don't run away from meee!"

It seemed that she had mistaken my astonishment for disgust. I wouldn't be put off just because she liked alcohol… But four twenty-four-ounce bottles, hmm… Wow.

Wait. Huh? Rewind. I feel like I just heard something momentous!

"…Ms. Saotome, you were a former *yuki onna* spirit?" I asked.

"What? Oh, yeah," she replied. "Didn't I mention?"

"First time I've heard it…," I said. "Did you know, Mr. Hoshino?"

"Mm-hmm, well, sure," he said, nodding like it was the most obvious thing in the world.

Are you serious? Hold on. Does that mean…?

"Could it be that you're also…?" I asked Mr. Hoshino.

…A former nonhuman?

"Nope. I've always been human," he responded.

"Oh. I see."

How anticlimactic.

I had been shocked by the bombshell Ms. Saotome had dropped, but considering her translucent skin and inhuman beauty, it wasn't difficult to accept the fact that she used to be a *yuki onna*.

"Come to think of it, I was drinking when we first met, right, Mr. Hoshino?" Ms. Saotome said.

"I had gotten lost in the mountains. There was snow all around me. Then I saw a woman dressed in a kimono holding a bottle of sake. I thought I had died."

"You're awful! But that was the moment I fell head over heels in love... Ha-ha, that sure takes me back."

Hmm?

"I was shocked when you followed me to the US; at least back then I was."

Hmm?

Something's going on here...

Ms. Saotome's cheeks grew red.

"Um, are the two of you...?" I hinted.

"We're married," Ms. Saotome said.

"Yep, married," Mr. Hoshino confirmed.

"Married?!" I exclaimed.

I had found out Mr. Hoshino was married because of the Handkerchief Incident, but who would've thought his partner was actually Ms. Saotome...?!

In that case, the handkerchief in question had been a present from Ms. Saotome, a present that I...

Now I get it...

I collapsed against Mr. Hoshino. Maybe the alcohol had rushed to my head all of a sudden.

"Mr. Hitoma? Mr. Hitoma!" Ms. Saotome cried. "Oh no, oh no! Is he okay?"

"...Let's give him some water," Mr. Hoshino said.

* * *

Have I matured this past year?
    With my head fogged by alcohol and drowsiness, I pondered the question in a daze.

    As a teacher.
    As a person.

To be honest, the answer wasn't immediately obvious.
    But I felt that I was now less resistant when it came to dealing with other people than before I came to this school.

    Is that because the students are nonhuman?
    Or is it because—

    —I hope everyone will be able to graduate next year?
    I hope all their dreams will come true?

    As if.

    Aaah, that's out of character for me.
    I'm not usually such a bleeding heart.
    The graduation ceremony made me feel warm and fuzzy.
    That's all.
    I'm sure of it.

Now then, no more indulging in sentiment.
    Life keeps on going. I'll continue living out my ordinary days.

And that out-of-character wish that had bubbled up inside me?
    I tucked it inside a corner of my heart for safekeeping.

    Time to go home and demolish my game backlog.

A **Misanthrope**
Teaches a Class for
Demi-Humans

Mr. Hitoma, Won't You Teach Us About Humans...?

Epilogue

A MISANTHROPE TEACHES A CLASS FOR DEMI-HUMANS

I was lost in the throes of battle, dressed in nothing but a tank top and my underwear. My joysticks were rattling up a storm.

"Booyah! Who's the champ?!" I cried.

I struck a victory pose, bringing my arms up to flex my biceps, but I inadvertently hit my elbow on the desk.

Whatever. It had been ages since I had a gaming marathon from morning to night. There was no better high than this.

A week after the graduation ceremony, I finally moved out of my parents' house, trading my cramped bedroom for a 1LDK apartment in the staff dormitory.

The bedroom was eight tatami mats and the living room was twelve, more than ample space for a single person. On top of that, the rent with gas, water, and electricity included was only 20,000 yen a month! It was almost too cheap... The cherry on top was my commute to school would be drastically easier.

Honestly, I had wanted to move earlier, but the timing hadn't been right. All the preparations before a move were a major hassle, and the whole thing was a pain in the neck.

Which was why I had been slowly packing up my things and getting my papers in order, and over spring break, I was able to move out at last.

Yes, I was living in the staff dorms, but I was excited to be living alone for the first time in a while.

Not to mention, I had a corner suite on the highest floor. On top of that, in a stroke of good fortune, the apartments next to and beneath me were empty, which was to say, I didn't have to worry about bothering people even if I was a little loud! To a gamer like me, that was a huge blessing!

"Geez... It's burning in here...," I groaned.

My blood was boiling. It'd been a while since I got so worked up. Between the heat radiating off my computer and the heat of my excitement, it felt like it was summer inside my room, even though spring had just begun.

I stood up and opened the window; it rattled as it slid in its sash. A cool breeze blew in from the outside world. The sun was blinding. It was a beautiful, clear day, and it seemed like it would be pleasantly warm in the sunlight.

"I should seize this chance and buy some ice cream," I said to myself.

The one downside to having moved into the dorms was that shopping was now a minor annoyance.

However, I could get online grocery orders delivered here with no problems, so for a heavy online shopper like me, it wasn't too inconvenient.

If I was to be picky, I do have one complaint. The delivery workers didn't actually come to my doorstep, but they delivered my order to the school storeroom, after which school staff brought it to the dorms. Therefore, the time between placing the order and getting my hands on the goods was longer than usual. Also, I could no longer make midnight trips to the convenience store. It was too far.

I stretched gently.

My stiff body cracked and popped from the small movement.

Man, I might regret it in the future if I don't at least take a walk once in a while.

There was no way I could leave the house in my current attire, so I put on a pair of shorts strewn on the bed and a shirt that had fallen on the floor. I had originally planned to wear sneakers, but it was too annoying to dig socks out of the cardboard box labeled *Clothing* lying in the corner of my room, so I made do with sandals.

The closest convenience store was three bus stops away. It took about twenty minutes on foot.

The weather's nice. I'll take a walk. I've been holed up at home playing games for two straight days. I have to move my body once in a while.

I left my apartment and walked down the stairs, yawning as I went.

Outside the dorms, the warm spring sunshine poured down on me. I went to my usual bus stop.

I wonder how Minazuki is doing.

Was she still busy preparing for her new life? I'd had a tough go of it the first time I lived by myself. It had been the fall of my second year in college. Figuring everything would be easier if I lived closer to my college, I'd embarked on my first experience living alone.

That was around when I got addicted to video games, if I remembered correctly. That was my first step down the road to becoming a true nerd.

I'm sure that from here on out, Minazuki will fall more and more in love with the things she enjoys.

Thoughts drifted through my head as I walked, and before I knew it, I was already at the cherry blossom tree by the barrier.

It's almost been a year since I first came here...

The flowers that had been buds on the day of the graduation ceremony were now in full bloom, just like the first time I'd laid eyes on them.

* * *

At my closest convenience store—which, again, was still three bus stops away—I bought Popsicles, newly released snacks, and cup noodles. Since I had come all the way here, I figured I should stock up, and I ended up buying an entire basket worth of food.

I left the store, eating one of the Popsicles I'd just bought as I headed back to the school.

The store was in a town, but the school was hidden in the forest. In this area, any signs of humanity quickly disappeared the moment you walked a little toward the forest.

Seriously, the forest is massive…

Maybe there was a shortcut that existed besides my usual road that the bus passed through.

My sense of adventure was tingling, but getting lost would be a problem, so I decided to go home the way I came.

I finished off my Popsicle and stuffed the garbage into a plastic bag.

The breeze was gentle and fresh.

Aaah… Yes, I should take a walk every so often. It feels oddly fulfilling, like I'm truly making the most of my vacation!

I strolled along the road in a chipper mood until I saw the bus stop closest to the school. I turned onto the lane branching off to the side.

I was about to pass the cherry blossom tree when I spotted something black squirming on the ground.

Thinking it strange, I walked up to it. The large shadow was around twenty inches long.

When I came closer, I saw golden eyes gleam from its face.

It was a black cat.

I must have startled it, for it jumped when it noticed me and dashed off.

I wonder if that cat is a student. Oh, but I'm still outside the barrier. Guess I'm wrong.

The black cat was content to stay as a black cat.

I hoped that was the case.

To be happy with the way you were, that was surely a blessing in and of itself.

I stared in the direction the cat had run off before continuing toward my new abode, with my bag of convenience store goods in hand.

* * *

I returned to the staff dorms to find Haneda sitting on the entrance stairs.

She waved at me casually.

"Hey, Mr. Hitoma. Welcome home."

"What are you doing here?" I said.

She was supposed to be enjoying her spring break, and instead she was here, wearing her usual getup.

"Hmm. 'Cause I wanted to see you," she said in her usual flippant tone.

Was she dodging the question?

"Did you have some business with me?" I asked.

"Wellll, I guess you could say that." She stood, dusted off her skirt, and came up to me. "Good job this last year, Mr. Hitoma. This school is probably completely different from your last one. How about it? Think you can stick it out here?"

"What kind of question is that? Are you my coworker or something?"

"Ah-ha-ha! I was just curious. So how was it?"

Come to think of it, she had asked me something similar when we first met...

The past year—there had been no shortage of challenges and hardships, times when I had no idea what to do and there had been no way out but through. However—

"You know," I replied, "it wasn't bad."

A gentle smile rose to Haneda's face. "I see. Good."

"...Huh? Was that your so-called business?"

"Yup, that's it! Oh, but I'm glad I got to see your cheerful face, even if it's lacking some color."

"Yeah, uh... It's the first time I've gone out in a while."

I had been playing games at home all this time.

What bad luck for Haneda to pay me a visit right when I was away. My rare excursion had caused her to wait...

"I got what I came for, so I should be off," Haneda said.

"Okay. Get home safe. See you in the new school year."

"See you. Later!" She headed off in the direction of the dorms.

I can't believe she went out of her way to ask me that one single question...

And that she knew I moved into staff housing in the first place.

Did she happen to see me moving in?

* * *

The next day, I went into school because I had some work to finish over spring break, and I was called into the principal's office.

The man was the same as always, but the strange art pieces in his office seemed to have multiplied.

First of all, the two bird statues by the entrance, aren't they a little... intimidating...? Cerberus wannabes. Were they here the last time I came...? They weren't, right...?

"I have an important person I wanted to introduce to you, Mr. Hitoma," the principal said. His tone was playful and his attire over-the-top, but even so, his demeanor was more rigid than usual.

Who could it be? A student? But would a student be considered an important person? I said nothing and waited for him to continue.

"The director," he finished.

The director.

The founder and proprietor of the school. The person responsible for it all.

I had been working at this school for nearly an entire year, but I hadn't ever met the director, or spoken to them virtually, or even seen a picture of them.

For that reason, I had begun to think they didn't exist in the first place... But they did.

"Um... Will the director be coming here now?" I asked.

Crap. I was wearing a cheap, shabby suit like I always did. I'd brushed my hair but nothing more. What if I had bedhead? My shoes weren't polished, and since I had to walk up the dirt path to school, they were muddy, too. They were pretty beat up...

The director won't think I'm being rude, will they?

"The director is in the office next door. We'll be going there immediately to introduce you."

That's too sudden! Please tell me things like this in advance! I can't do anything about my bargain suits, but I might have been able to make myself more presentable at least...!

Quite frankly, I had forgotten the director's office even existed.

It was right next to the principal's office. I hadn't ever set foot inside, and it was tucked into the corner of the school building. I had dismissed it as none of my business.

"Y-yes, sir."

We're going right now…

The principal's lips quirked upward at my reluctant acceptance, and he directed me toward the boardroom.

It's my first time coming here…

The two of us lined up in front of the room, and the principal knocked on the door. A female voice called out, "Come in."

The principal opened the door and gestured for me to go in.

I'm so nervous…

The director is inside… What kind of person is she? She does seem to be a woman judging by her voice, but what should I do if she's another jolly eccentric, like the female version of the principal…? Agh, it's definitely possible…

"Pardon me." I entered the room and bowed deeply.

At that moment, I found myself enveloped by warmth. Whether or not it was because the heat was turned on, it seemed to be more humid than in the principal's room.

So muggy…

Actually, it's practically burning *in here.*

"It's nice to meet you, Mr. Hitoma."

The director greeted me.

I had been too nervous to notice before, but this voice…

She had said, "Nice to meet you," but this was hardly the first time we had met.

I'd heard this voice the day prior.

It couldn't be, I thought and raised my head.

The person in front of me was in her uniform, sitting on the desk with her legs crossed as if we were in the middle of a break between periods.

* * *

"Thanks for yesterday. It made me happy to hear you feel positively about this school."

Sitting in front of me was an advanced student who I had spent the last year with.

Tobari Haneda capped off her words with a satisfied grin.

* * *

"Ah, is my appearance causing you trouble?" Haneda asked.

She hopped off the desk with a quiet "hup" and landed on the rug. At that instant, tall flames of red and orange enveloped her body.

"Whoa! Haneda…?!" I cried, shaken up by the roaring campfire that had appeared out of nowhere and the wave of heat.

But soon, it disappeared like it had never been there. Standing where Haneda had been was a grown woman who closely resembled her.

She was about the same height as me with a glamorous hourglass figure. Her orange hair was long and silky and curled upward at the ends. Clothed in a bold, glitzy red dress, she looked like a Hollywood celebrity.

"Ah-ha-ha, that shocked look on your face is pure gold, Mr. Hitoma!" the woman said, laughing at my bewilderment.

Her voice, her gestures, and even her laugh were exactly the same as Tobari Haneda's.

Which meant—

"I understand how surprised you must be, Mr. Hitoma!" the principal said. "For someone you have thought of as your student the entire time to actually be the director, what a shocking development! Let me introduce you once again! This is the director of this fine establishment, Ms. Shiranui!"

"Sorry to surprise you! I take that form so I can observe the students up close. It's also to help me decide whether a new teacher should continue working at this school."

The chaotic turn of events had brought the gears in my head to a grinding halt.

"Um…D-Director Shiranui…? How should I conduct myself around you going forward…?" I asked.

"Oh, yes, the same as before, please! I'll be posing as Tobari next year, too," she said. "But seriously, sorry I kept it from you."

"It's fine… I mean, I know you had your reasons, but…"

I was still muddled by the suddenness of it all.

Tobari Haneda was a fake identity.

She was actually the director of the school.

She disguised herself to observe the school's day-to-day activities from the front lines.

If I thought about it really carefully, even though Haneda had always seemed lackadaisical, she had always been attuned to the rhythms of the class—and to me.

In a corner of my mind, there was a part of me that had always marveled at how brazenly she stepped into my affairs for a student.

Inside me, a puzzle piece snapped into place.

I see. Haneda—Director Shiranui—has been by my side, watching over me, all this time.

"Let me tell you, my boy! The director is a phoenix! The ultimate being who presides over everything in this world!" the principal declared.

A phoenix.

A mythical creature often depicted in stories as an all-powerful deus ex machina.

The barrier around the school, the mysterious gems, the human transformation… Even for a school for demi-humans, the setting was a little *too* fantasy-like. I had grown immune to it, but without a first-tier cheat like a phoenix, such circumstances would be impossible.

Then the principal revealed, "I am actually a crow *tengu*!"

That explains everything!!

I'd always thought he was outlandish, so I had been mentally prepared, but it was still shocking to hear.

"I can see fragments one month into the future! That's why I knew you would work hard at this school!" he said. "Actually, that was one of the reasons we hired you!"

Precognition... The principal's basically a living cheat code...

"Oh, that's right, Mr. Hitoma," the director said. "Thanks for the other day."

"What day...?" I asked.

"Um, back around November? I think it was? The time I was ill."

Ah, that sounds vaguely familiar.

"Have I jogged your memory? That was a rough season for me. I had my hands full with the preparations for the new students," she said.

"You have to oversee that yourself?" I asked.

"In fact, it's a job only I can do. I have to personally confirm each applicant's objective and determine whether they would be a good fit for the school. If I think they should be admitted, with my powers, I modify the barrier so it'll transform the student into a demi-human and bring them to the school."

The director turned her blue eyes on me.

"Quite frankly, I built this school on a whim, but it's become quite amusing. It's fun watching mortal beings give living their all. I enjoy it."

Phoenixes lived forever.

That much was true in any story.

"My ultimate goal is to obtain a finite life span," the director told me. Her voice was soft and melancholy, but in some strange way, it was also warm. "Watching everyone, I started to think that I, too, would like to live in this world in order to die."

To live to die. How fitting a phrase. Every living being would one day die. We lived day after day to our fullest to ensure we would not leave behind any regrets.

"When that time comes, I'll have let go of everything, finished all that I want to do, and can leave with an untroubled heart. It won't be until way, way in the future! Ah-ha-ha! I doubt I'll be able to accomplish it in your lifetime, Mr. Hitoma..." She gazed out the window with a faraway look in her eyes.

I wondered how long she had been alive.

That day, like always, she carried us mortal beings on her back, time flowing around her.

The director opened her mouth slowly.
"Say, Mr. Hitoma. Do you like humans?" she asked me nonchalantly, as if we were just shooting the breeze.

Do I like humans?

Humans are selfish. Uncaring about others.
They exploit the good in bad faith and take the honest as fools.

"I hate them," I said.

That hadn't changed.
However...

The human who had shown Minazuki the dance of a lifetime.
The other human half of Oogami.
The human who was Usami's precious friend.
And lastly, the humans Haneda knew were mortal through and through.

Those were humans seen from perspectives completely different from my own.
Humans were egotistical, emotional to a fault, cuffed by reality, and fragile.
But they were also independent, overflowing with words, free to chase grand dreams, and lived to the fullest in the time they had.

"I still hate humans, but that feels fine the way it is for now."

The way it is for now.
I decided to value how I felt about humans first and foremost.

Instead of forcing myself to like them, first, I wanted to meet myself where I was at.

Until the day when I learned to like humans.
Until the day when I learned to like myself.
That was my first step.

The director smiled benevolently at me as if she knew exactly what I was thinking.

This is Shiranui High School.
A school in the middle of the woods where nonhumans study.

A place that feels like a different world but isn't.
In this corner of our humdrum world, we'll keep on living our lives.

Afterword

Hello! Debut author Kurusu Natsume here! It's nice to meet you!

Thank you so much for picking up my first book, *A Misanthrope Teaches a Class for Demi-Humans*!!

I've liked reading stories ever since I was little, so I started writing them myself. I'm blessed to have this opportunity to publish one of my books. It is truly an honor. I couldn't have done it without the support of the publishing team, as well as everyone who believed in me. Thank you!!

While we're here, I would like to share how *A Class for Demi-Humans* came to be.

The impetus came during one of my usual live streams. A short story I wrote in a certain game caught the eye of my now editor, who said to me, "Natsume! Won't you try writing long-form fiction?!"

When I actually put pen to paper, I was surprised by how *right* it felt...!! Like I was writing the perfect story at the perfect time. It's just a personal anecdote, but you never know when inspiration will strike. That's life...or so I think.

And born from that spark was *A Class for Demi-Humans*!

Once I began, my pen flew across the page!!

Originally, my editor told me, "Since this is your first time writing a novel, do your best and try to hit 100,000 characters!" However, I was having so much fun, somehow, my first draft ended up being almost 150,000 characters. How bizarre!

Therefore, in order to stay under the page limit, with tears in my eyes,

I erased several scenes…! I had to work particularly hard to edit the prologue where Hitoma appears.

How did you enjoy the book…?! I was terribly grateful that the book attracted far more attention than I had anticipated even before it was released. I was nervous whether I could meet such high expectations, but I hope you were satisfied by the story…!

Our protagonist, Hitoma, was neither transported into another world nor reincarnated; he was born and raised in the same world we live in. He has gone through a lot and has some flaws, but I would be happy if you welcome him with love and affection.

I would like to move on to acknowledgments.

Number one! A big thanks to Sai Izumi, who provided the fantastic illustrations, setting, and character designs!! While honoring the vision I had in my head, they created polished and lovely designs for the characters! Hitoma's lethargy! Usami's sass! Tobari's leadership spirit! Kyouka's sweetness! Isaki's timidity and Full-Moon Isaki's wild-child energy (and the gap between the two)! They are all the best! My original designs are included at the end of this volume, so I hope you will enjoy the comparison!

I would also like to thank my editor, who always gave me advice when I ran up against my inexperience as a writer. In addition, thanks to my manager who, given my circumstances, dedicated their time to accompany me in my meetings with my editor.

In addition, my heartfelt thanks to the illustrators who worked on the special in-store displays. To Hitsuji Maki for the amazing artwork featuring Isaki and Tobari in the nighttime. To Misumi for the artwork with a trendy and adorable Kyouka and Isaki partying it up. To Sakura Kurihara for the artwork with Isaki and Usami cooking together, all the more cute for their clumsiness. To Vane for the artwork of Kyouka and Tobari with a warmth that can be felt through the page. To Ui Shigure for the artwork of Usami and Kyouka, charming in their comfy pajamas. Thank you all very much!

*   *   *

Actually, each chapter in this volume was spun from three audience-suggested prompts! Did you notice? Maybe…?!

Thank you to everyone who provided the prompts: Amamiya Kokoro, Ange Katrina, Gwelu Os Gar, Shirayuki Tomoe, Nui Sociere, Mashiro Meme, Yashiro Kizuku, Yamagami Karuta, Ryushen, and my Natsumate!

You gifted me with words that were unknown to me before and, in doing so, added a wonderful spice to the story. Thank you!

Last but not least! I would like to thank someone who has supported me all this time—or who will generously give me their all going forward: you. Thank *you*!! I'm lucky to have been bestowed with so many fortunes, and I hope to return the favor a bit at a time through my writing in the future.

To that end!! I'm going to live a long life!! Live long with me!!

Now then! Thank you for reading until this point!!

I look forward to meeting you again!

Kurusu Natsume
February 2022

Rei Hitoma

▼ Kurusu Natsume's Vision

"I...wonder if I can learn to like humans in this school full of nonhumans."

▼ Kurusu Natsume's Vision

"It's a pleasure to make your acquaintance! My name is Kyouka Minazuki!"

Isaki Oogami

"Oh, um... I'm next...I guess...?"

"Your heart's racing 'cause I'm so adorable. I get it. Yep!"

▼ Kurusu Natsume's Vision

Sai Izumi's Character Design

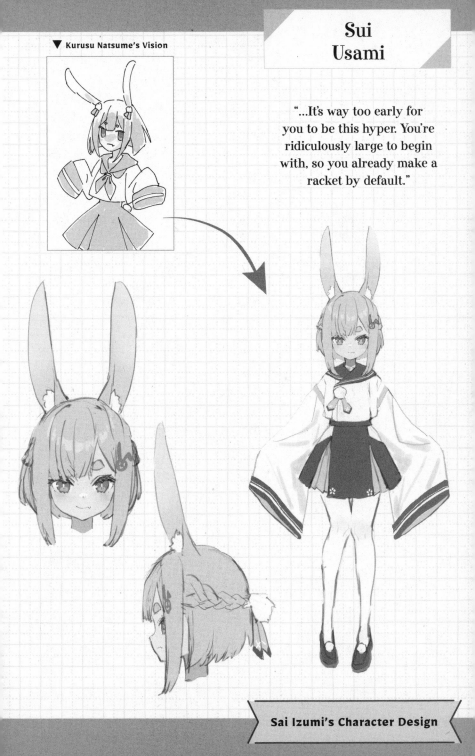

▼ Kurusu Natsume's Vision

Sui
Usami

"...It's way too early for you to be this hyper. You're ridiculously large to begin with, so you already make a racket by default."

Sai Izumi's Character Design

Tobari
Haneda

"I'm into music. I'll listen
to basically anything."

Sai Izumi's Character Design

Yuki Saotome

▼ Kurusu Natsume's Vision

"The students all call me Ms. Yuki! Feel free to call me that, too, Mr. Hitoma!"

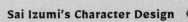

Sai Izumi's Character Design

Satoru Hoshino

"It's been a few weeks since you started. How is everything? Used to it yet?"

▼ Kurusu Natsume's Vision

▼ Kurusu Natsume's Vision

"Mm, it's only natural that you find me suspicious."

Sai Izumi's Character Design

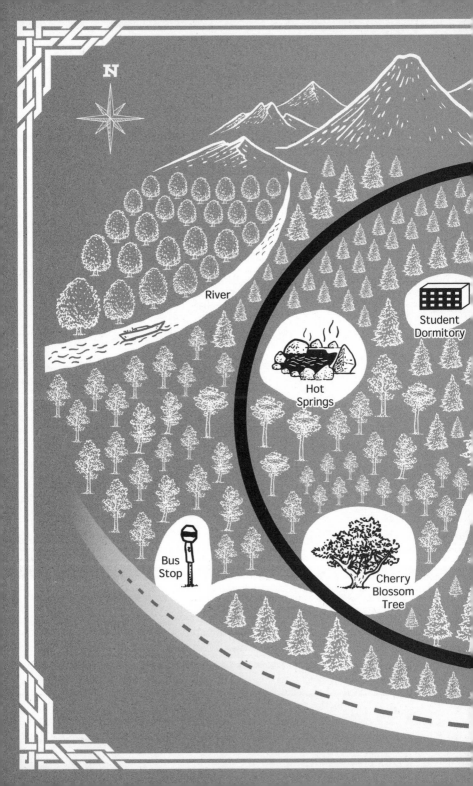

Campus Map

Gymnasium

Annex

Main Building

Field

Barrier

Staff Dormitory

Main Building Floor Plan

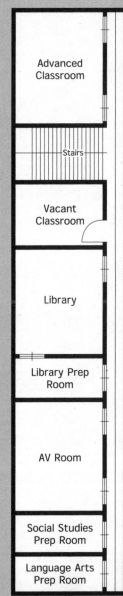

Annex Music Room • Art Room • School Store • Computer Lab • AV Room Home Ec • Culinary Arts

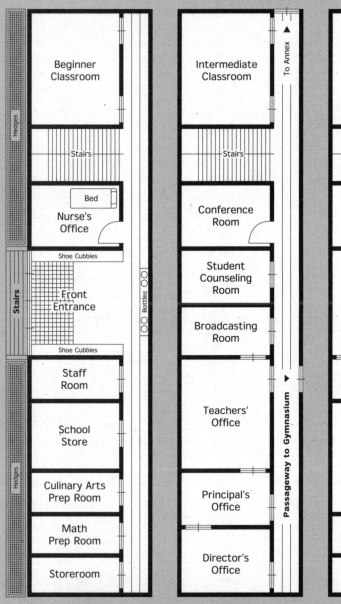

1F

- Beginner Classroom
- Stairs
- Nurse's Office — Bed
- Shoe Cubbies
- Front Entrance
- Shoe Cubbies
- Bottles
- Staff Room
- School Store
- Culinary Arts Prep Room
- Math Prep Room
- Storeroom
- Hedges
- Stairs

2F

- Intermediate Classroom
- To Annex
- Stairs
- Conference Room
- Student Counseling Room
- Broadcasting Room
- Teachers' Office
- Principal's Office
- Director's Office
- Passageway to Gymnasium

3F

- Advanced Classroom
- Stairs
- Vacant Classroom
- Library
- Library Prep Room
- AV Room
- Social Studies Prep Room
- Language Arts Prep Room

A Misanthrope Teaches a Class for Demi-Humans

Mr. Hitoma, Won't You Teach Us About Humans...?

Author

Kurusu Natsume

Illustrator

Sai Izumi

Editor

Suguru Ohtake

··

Special Thanks

Chapter Prompts Contributors

Prologue	The Misanthrope and the Classroom of Destiny
Mashiro Meme (zebra, eyelash, wax figure)	**Gwelu Os Gar** (pop-ups to the catcher, "Soran Bushi," top of the class at Harvard)
The Misanthrope and the Crown of Foam	**The Misanthrope and the Lonely Castle on a Full Moon's Night**
Amamiya Kokoro (fish cake, warden's privileges, "Tomorrow")	**Shirayuki Tomoe** (cod roe, papaya, hyaluronic acid)
The Misanthrope and the Summer Vacation by the River	**The Misanthrope and the Angel's Comet**
Ryushen (signpost, watermelon, pillow)	**Ange Katrina** (Calpico, angel, caterpillar fungus)
The Misanthrope and Tobari's Hymn	**The Misanthrope and the Light of Dawn**
Yamagami Karuta (otoMAD, let's get out of here, stomachache)	**Yashiro Kizuku** (seaweed, Gotemba, *Wreck*ng Crew*)
The Misanthrope and the Long-Awaited Graduation Ceremony	**Epilogue**
Natsumate (720ml bottle of alcohol, gas heater, ring)	**Nui Sociere** (Popsicle, black cat, tank top)

A **Misanthrope** Teaches a Class for **Demi-Humans**

Mr. Hitoma, Won't You Teach Us About Humans...?

A Day in the Life of Rei Mitoma -Day-off Version- by Kurusu Natsume

A MISANTHROPE TEACHES A CLASS FOR DEMI-HUMANS